REBEL

★ RAIDERS ★

LISA TRIMBLE ACTOR

To Barbara,
Enjoy this mostly
true Story!
Lisa T. Actor
5-14-13

Illustrations by Hazel Mitchell
(www.hazelmitchell.com)

Wasteland Press
www.wastelandpress.net
Shelbyville, KY USA

Rebel Raiders
by Lisa Trimble Actor
www.rebelraiders.us

First Printing – March 2013
ISBN: 978-1-60047-835-2
Library of Congress Control Number: 2013932685

Illustrations by Hazel Mitchell
www.hazelmitchell.com

Printed in the U.S.A.

0   1   2   3   4   5   6   7   8   9   10   11

For my father, Robert G. Trimble, who taught me to love words.
For my mother, Barbara G. Trimble, who encouraged my writing.

And to my husband, David I. Actor, for his steadfast love.

CHAPTER ONE

Anyone living in Jackson County in 1863 knew, without a doubt, that the top of Cemetery Hill was the surest spot this side of the Ohio River to catch a refreshing breeze. The hilltop graveyard was everyone's favorite place for springtime kite flying, summertime picnicking or watching a golden sunset on a late autumn evening.

On this particular afternoon, Dill Dunbar stood among eight freshly dug graves wishing for the barest hint of a breeze. There were no kites dancing at the ends of silver strings. No quilted blankets spread out for picnics. Not a single leaf rustled in the old sycamore.

Dill was there for the other reason folks came to this grassy hillside. To bury the dead.

Dill scrambled over the dirt pile beside Uncle Swinge's grave. Her stomach felt like she'd swallowed a rotten apple. This dark hole could not be her uncle's final resting spot. Graves were for corpses, not handsome, young soldiers.

Ma's sobs joined the cries rising up to heaven from the families awaiting their soldiers' coffins. Dill wiped her eyes. The undertaker's mules had just begun their long, plodding march up Cemetery Hill. At this rate, it would be sunset before her uncle's body was laid to rest.

"That ain't your uncle's grave," said a voice.

Dill pinched her nose. She recognized the voice of Simon Harrison, the smelliest boy in all of Jackson County. Her friend hadn't taken a bath since his ma had passed away from diphtheria back in February. By May, when school had let out, Simon had stunk worse than Doc Miller's old Billy goat. Now that it was summer, folks in town crossed the street when they saw him coming.

"Of course this is his grave," said Dill.

Simon heaved a dirt clod at the hole in the ground. "I'll bet you a penny it ain't." He nodded at the wooden grave marker. "Did you see the name written on the cross?"

Dill swallowed hard. Simon would never bet real money unless he knew he could win. She climbed back over the dirt pile to read the letters printed on the cross.

Elmer Wellington
Sgt, Ohio 53rd Inf, Co E
Died July 10, 1863
Age twenty years, eleven months, fourteen days

Dill frowned. The age was right. So was the last name. But her uncle's first name was Swinge, not Elmer.

"Read the names on the other crosses," said Simon. "Not a Swinge among 'em."

Dill weaved in and out of the mourners, inspecting all eight graves. Simon was right. Uncle Swinge's name didn't appear on a single wooden cross.

"What do you reckon this means?" Dill asked when she'd circled back.

Simon ran his fingers through his greasy hair. "Only one thing it can mean," he said thoughtfully. "Your uncle ain't dead."

Dill flipped her braids over her shoulders. The weight hanging from her heart felt lighter. Could Simon be right? She grabbed his ragged shirtsleeve and pulled him to the cedar grove where her brother stood in the shade, talking with the preacher.

Reverend Loxley's coat hung from a broken-off branch. Rings of sweat soaked his shirt around the armpits. "How did your uncle die?" he asked Jim.

"Shot in the belly by a Minié," said Dill's brother.

The preacher let out a low whistle. "A Minié ball to the gut?"

Dill tugged on Jim's hand. "Uncle Swinge ain't dead," she said.

Jim scowled. "Can't you see I'm talking?"

Dill stomped her foot. She was nearly eleven and hated being treated like a child. Ever since Jim had turned sixteen he'd acted more like her pa than her brother. "There's no grave for Uncle Swinge!" she shouted.

Jim gave the preacher a polite smile. "I showed you his grave," he hissed at Dill. "It's over there, next to Ma."

"But that cross says Elmer," said Dill.

Jim shook his head. "Swinge was a nickname. His real name was Elmer, like your name is Cordelia."

The rotten apple in Dill's stomach grew to melon-size. She had never known she'd had an Uncle *Elmer*, and now he was dead.

CHAPTER TWO

The mules inched past the sweet gums, sycamores, and maples. At last they rolled to a stop between the cedars. A dove called, low and mournful, as soldiers dressed in blue unloaded pinewood coffins.

Dill's eyes burned from holding back tears. "Uncle Swinge's coffin is nailed shut," she whispered to Jim. "How do we know it's him inside?"

"We know it's him on account of Ma got his tag."

"What tag?"

"The one with his name and the names of his next of kin. Soldiers write these things on paper and pin them inside their uniforms, in case they're killed in battle."

A memory filled up Dill's head. She had watched Pa write their names on a piece of paper before he'd marched off to war.

Alexander Dunbar of Jackson, Ohio.
Husband to Susannah. Father to James and Cordelia.

"In case I become too befuddled to find my way home," Pa had said to Dill before pinning the paper into his pocket.

Now Dill knew the truth. Pa had wanted his body sent home, in case he was killed. Hot tears filled her eyes. She hated this war.

Once all the coffins were in the ground, the preacher stepped in front of the graves. He raised his hand as if to direct a choir. But there was no choir. Just a handful of soldiers and soldiers' kin. They knew the funeral hymn by heart.

Low in the grave he lay,
Jesus my savior.
Waiting the coming day,
Jesus my Lord.
He arose! He arose!
Hallelujah! Christ arose!

Reverend Loxley opened his Bible and started in on his funeral sermon. Dill had heard enough about death. She left the clump of mourners and lit out for the top of Cemetery

Hill. Simon took off after her, making Dill break into a dog trot. She trotted past the Tiltons, Wisemans and McKitricks. At the Jones family plot, she turned to face the preacher who was waving his arms skyward.

Simon stopped a short distance away. He pulled up a blade of grass from beside the headstone of Primilla B. Jones and stuck the tender end in his mouth. "Promise you won't tell nobody if I show you something?" he asked.

Before Dill could answer, Simon shoved his hand into his pocket. When he pulled out his fist and opened his fingers, a piece of lead the size of a shooter marble lay in his palm.

Dill plucked the chunk of lead from Simon's hand. "It's a Minié ball, ain't it?"

"Yep," said Simon, grinning. "Wickedest shot ever forged."

Dill studied the piece of lead. It was longer than any shot she had held, heavier too; and it was tapered at one end, like a candle. She turned it over to inspect the blunt end. "It's hollow," she said.

Simon nodded. "That's what makes the Minié so deadly." He took the Minié ball back from Dill. "See how it's round in the middle, before narrowing at the tip?"

Dill looked closer. Sure enough; the Minié had a bulge in its belly, like a chubby little boy.

"The Rebels pack the hollow core with gunpowder," said Simon. "When the hammer strikes the back it lights the gunpowder. The heat makes the middle swell up 'til it completely fills the gun barrel. That tight fit makes a Minié ball shoot faster and farther than any other lead shot."

A shiver slid down Dill's spine. "A Minié ball killed my uncle," she said.

"Not surprising," said Simon. "They can rip through a man standing a quarter mile off, killing him and the fellow behind him, too. And the moment it hits him – *bang!* – blows his guts clear outside his body."

Dill felt sick. "That's gruesome," she said.

Simon hurled the Minié against a headstone. Dill ran over and picked it out of the grass. "Why didn't it blow?" she asked, handing the piece of lead back to Simon.

"The Rebels fired this one months ago. It didn't hit nobody or it'd be all tore up."

"Where did you get such a thing?"

"My brother, Ben, picked it up at Shiloh. He sent it to me, along with some arrowheads he found on the battlefield."

Dill shook her head. "Poor Uncle Swinge. No wonder they nailed his coffin shut."

"Makes sense," said Simon. "Can't show off a man whose guts are blown outside his body."

The locusts hummed in the trees beside the Jones family plot. Under the cedars, the preacher's booming voice rose above the locusts' drone. "Yea, though I walk through the valley of the shadow of death, I will fear no evil, for thou art with me, thy rod and thy staff they comfort me."

"Amen," said a chorus of voices. A soldier raised a bugle to his lips. His notes hung slow and sad over the graveyard, like a long, black curtain.

"What's that song?" asked Dill.

"That's Taps," said Simon. "It means the soldiers' day is done."

Dill stuck her fingers in her ears. She never wanted to hear that song again. When the bugle was finished, she pulled up a blade of grass and tasted it. "How do you know so much about war, Simon?"

"I come up here for all the Union burials." Simon scratched his chin. "See that man with the tall, black hat? Do you know who he is?"

"He looks a bit like Doc Miller, but I know he ain't because he doesn't have a mustache," Dill flicked the grass over a headstone.

"That's Mr. Dickason. He keeps track of the county's money," said Simon. "His son was buried up here last week. A Rebel cannon ball knocked his head clean off. They buried his head in its own box, beside his body."

Dill frowned. "You made that up."

"No I didn't," said Simon. He pointed to a spot down the hill. "I can show you the two graves." He looked into Dill's brown eyes. "This war is ugly," he said. "The Rebels'll stop at nothing to make us Yankees suffer."

Dill scrambled on top of a limestone slab with the name JONAH C. JONES carved in its side. She had heard enough about war. "I'll bet you can see all of Jackson from up here," she said, looking down on the town.

"You can see more than that," said Simon. He pointed a finger to the west. "See that hill away off yonder?"

"Which one?" asked Dill. Southern Ohio was full of wooded hills and valleys, one right after the other, like oversized folds of fluffy, green flannel.

"Beyond Salt Lick Creek. Past Big Rock Ridge. Can ya see it?"

Dill laid her head on Simon's arm and shut one eye until she was looking straight down his pointing finger. "The one with the fuzzy round top?"

"Yep," said Simon. "That's Pike Hill."

Dill lifted her head. "Way out by Piketon? In Pike County?"

Simon nodded. "Don't the dead have the best view in Jackson?"

Dill sighed. "Closest you can get to heaven."

The apple in her stomach shrunk to cherry size. Poor Uncle Swinge would never know he had the best view in all of Jackson County.

CHAPTER THREE

Eight patches of dirt scarred the green earth between the cedar trees. Dill watched Ma kneel to lay a bouquet of forest violets beside Uncle Swinge's cross. In the shade of the giant sycamore, Jim had joined a crowd gathered around the county treasurer. Dill wandered over to see what was happening.

"General Morgan skirted our Union forces on the north side of Cincinnati," said Mr. Dickason. "He fooled the governor by sending telegrams to Columbus, ordering his men north. Then he sent his army east." Mr. Dickason removed his top hat and wiped his forehead with a handkerchief. "John Hunt Morgan is fixing to raid clear across Ohio."

"We've got five counties between us and Cincinnati," said Mr. Landrum, the barrel-chested man who ran the granary by the train depot. "Surely they'll be stopped before they reach Jackson."

"Don't bet on it," said Mr. Dickason. "They've left a path of destruction across Indiana. The Hoosier militias were no match for 'em."

"The Union Army will catch them," said the widow Johnson. Her husband, Tommy, had been laid to rest the week before with the county treasurer's son.

Mr. Dickason shook his head. "Morgan's men are setting fire to every bridge they cross. It's making them hard to catch."

"What's Governor Tod doing to protect us?" demanded a gentleman in a long waistcoat.

A murmur rippled through the crowd. Mr. Dickason raised his hand until the rumbling stopped. "The governor has called for a state militia. Fifty-five thousand men have already reported for duty in Columbus. They'll ride south tomorrow."

"But Columbus is three days' ride from here," shouted the widow Johnson. "They'll never reach us in time."

"They've got the fastest horses in central Ohio," said Mr. Dickason. "Regardless, the governor is asking every citizen to prepare for war." He stuck his hat on his head with a tap. "Hurry home. Load your rifles. Bury your silver."

Dill tugged on her brother's shirtsleeve. "Can we go?" she whispered.

Jim nodded. "Let's collect Ma."

Overhead, the sycamore leaves rustled. A branch cracked, and Simon Harrison fell to the ground with a *whump*. Dill shook her head. Leave it to Simon to make a fool of himself at such an important time.

CHAPTER FOUR

Long shadows criss-crossed the lane as Ol' Luke pulled the wagon along the western side of Cemetery Hill. Ma sat beside Jim, her back rigid as a cedar plank. "What's this Rebel's name again?" she asked.

"Morgan," said Jim.

"General John Hunt Morgan," added Dill.

Ma twisted her handkerchief around her fingers. "And what does he want with the likes of us?"

"He means to give us a taste of war," said Jim.

Ma pondered that notion. "Well I never heard of the like. And while your pa is fighting at Vicksburg. How will we defend ourselves?"

"The Ohio militia may stop 'em," said Dill.

Jim jiggled the reins. "It's doubtful," he said.

Ma sighed. "Let's pray someone stops them before they reach Jackson."

Ol' Luke turned off the main road. A bark rang out from the tree-lined lane followed by a high-pitched howl. Dill hopped to the ground. Nellie the one-eyed beagle raced down the lane like she'd been shot from a cannon.

The little beagle had found her way to the Dunbar farm in a snowstorm two winters back, in spite of having just one good eye. It had taken Dill three days to convince Ma they should keep her. Pa had pitched in, too. The way he'd figured it, the beagle's ears and nose would more than make up for the loss of an eye.

Nellie had proven Pa right. She could hear a wagon turn up the lane before anyone ever caught sight of it from the house.

Dill ran her hand down the beagle's spotted back.

"Get to your evening chores," Ma said from the wagon. "We'll have a late supper."

Dill hurried inside to take off her Sunday clothes and shoes. She pulled on her blue dress and pinafore before running to the well to fill Nellie's dented water pan.

"Let's find Jim," said Dill, after the beagle had lapped her fill.

Nellie led the way up the well-worn path to the barn. Ol' Luke stood in the fenced yard, swatting flies with his tail. Nellie stopped outside the barn door and waited for Dill to lift the latch. A pack of cats froze in the evening sun. But Nellie wasn't hunting cats. She trotted past empty horse stalls to the far side of the barn.

Sure enough; there was Jim in the outer lot, a yellow straw dangling from his lips. Before him stood the buckskin stallion Pa had bought from Simon's pa before going off to war. Mr. Harrison was known for raising the fastest horses in Southeastern Ohio. Pa's purchase of such a fine stallion meant he expected Jim to pass into manhood while he was away.

Jim had looked six inches taller the morning he'd led the horse up their lane. "His name is Buckeye," he'd said to Dill, "for the Buckeye state of Ohio."

Buck had pranced and thrown his black mane in the air. "He's feisty," said Dill.

"You bet he is," said Jim. "He's of the flyer class. Like riding lightning."

"When can I ride?" Dill had asked.

"Not 'til I say he's broke," said Jim.

For over a year, Dill had waited for the day when Jim would boost her on the stallion's back to gallop across the meadow and race along the cornfield.

"Can I ride him tonight?" Dill asked.

Buck pushed his muzzle into Jim's chest. "No," said Jim.

Dill reached into the tattered bag tied to her brother's belt. She lifted an oat kernel between her thumb and forefinger. Buck picked it up with the lips of a lamb. "He's so gentle," she said. "One of these days, I'm going to leap on his back and ride."

Jim glared down at Dill. "Like you did last night?"

Dill stared back.

Jim's jaw muscle tightened. "I saw your footprints in the mud. You came out in last night's storm."

Dill glanced down at Buck's dark hooves. "The thunder woke me up," she said. "I came out to check on him."

"In your nightgown?"

"In Pa's old work shirt."

"And you rode him."

"I didn't." Dill ran her fingers down Buck's soft muzzle. "He threw me off before I could get a hold of his mane."

Jim grabbed Dill by the shoulders and looked her straight in the eye. "Don't you ride without my permission, d'ya hear?"

"I'm tired of waiting." Dill tried to wiggle loose. "And, besides, I don't want Simon to have the first ride."

Jim loosened his grip. "What makes you think Simon will ride before you?"

"He's telling folks he gets the first ride," Dill said, "since his pa raised Buck."

"I'll see that you ride before Simon," said Jim. The tightness in his jaw smoothed out a bit. "But stay off, 'til I say it's time. Ya hear?"

Dill poked Jim in the side. "Promise you won't tell Ma I tried to ride. She'll take a switch to my back side if she finds out."

A grin flickered across Jim's lips. "I ought to tell her. But I won't," he said. "Besides, I'm thinking of riding off to join the militia."

"On Buck?" asked Dill.

"Of course," Jim grinned.

"Ma would never allow it. She already said as much. When Pa joined the Union Army she said they already had her brother and her husband. They weren't getting her son."

"The Ohio militia is different," said Jim. "It's a civilian force."

"You could still get shot by a Rebel."

Jim ran his hand down Buck's long nose. "Not if I'm riding him," he said. "He's faster than any of Mr. Harrison's other horses. Besides, I'm sixteen now. I don't need Ma's permission."

"Try telling her," said Dill.

Jim shook his head. "I'll never get off this farm." He nodded toward the barn. "I brought the pails from the house. Get to the milking while I clean out stalls."

Dill scooted a stool up to Sadie. She pushed her head into the cow's soft belly and pulled down hard on her teats. Twin streams of milk sang against the bottom of the bucket.

Three black and white kittens popped out from between the hay piles and lined up across from Sadie. A spotted kitten with a bent whisker stood up on his hind legs. "Meow!" he demanded.

Dill squirted milk at the bossy kitten. He caught the first squirt on his tongue. The second hit him square in the nose, causing him to sneeze milk across the other kittens. The surprise on the kittens' faces was so funny, Dill stopped milking and laughed out loud.

Across the barn, Jim tossed fresh straw into Buck's stall. His jaw muscle was so tight, it bulged out in a knot.

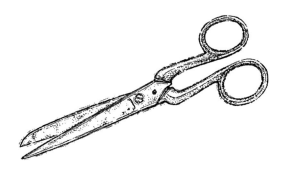

CHAPTER FIVE

The next morning, Dill got up before the sun lit the top of Cemetery Hill. Jim's bed was empty. She reached under her mattress and felt for something she'd hidden the day before. It was Pa's old work shirt. And it was still wet. She tossed it into the willow wash basket.

Jim's clothes lay in a heap at the foot of his bed - a pair of soiled britches and two dirty work shirts. Dill threw the clothes into the basket and scooted it into the kitchen. Ma was pulling a pan of biscuits from the hearth. Her eyes had lost the redness from the day before, but her cheeks still carried a few pink blotches.

Dill pushed the basket to a spot beside the door. She smothered a hot biscuit with molasses. She had barely bit into the biscuit when Nellie's howl rose up from the front of the house.

Ma touched the puffy skin beneath her eyes. "Oh dear," she said. "I'm not ready for company."

Dill tore through the front door. The sun's rays crested Cemetery Hill as she leapt to the porch rail. "It's Mr. Harrison," she called. "He's got Simon with him."

Jeremiah Harrison drove his team up the lane at lightning speed. Simon stood on the bench beside him, leaning into the wind, like a hawk riding an air current.

Mr. Harrison pulled his horses to a halt in front of Ma's vegetable garden. The sudden stop sent Simon flying. He rolled head over heels through the dirt, not stopping until he'd reached the second row of sweet corn. He leapt to his feet, picked a tomato off the vine and bowed to the string beans, like they were a circus audience cheering his stunt.

Jim laughed out loud from beside the rain barrel.

Quick as a rabbit, Simon leapt to the porch to offer Ma her own tomato. Ma set the tomato on the rail and took Simon by the shoulders. "Get my scissors," she said to Dill.

"No haircuts!" shouted Simon. He rolled his eyes at his pa. But Mr. Harrison was too busy talking with Jim to notice.

Dill grabbed the scissors from the quilting basket and slapped them into her mother's palm. "I'll trim just enough to see your blue eyes," said Ma, snipping Simon's raggedy bangs. When she had finished in front, she turned Simon around and trimmed the back until his hair no longer hung across his collar. "You'd be a handsome boy if you'd wash your face now and then," she said, turning him back around.

Dill dropped a wet rag in her mother's hand. Ma scrubbed Simon's cheeks until the freckles showed through. "Your mother is rolling in her grave at the sight of you," she said.

Jim's work boots clunked on the front steps. "I'm riding Buck to town with Mr. Harrison," he said.

Ma let go of Simon's chin. "What?" she asked. "But he's still too wild."

"Buck's broke?" asked Simon.

"Pert near," said Jim, smiling.

Simon clapped his hands. "I want a ride."

Dill pushed Simon aside. "Jim says I get the first ride."

Ma threw her hands in the air. "No one's riding that devil of a horse if I have anything to say about it." She laid a hand on Jim's shoulder. "You may ride to town," she said. "In Mr. Harrison's wagon."

"Aw, Ma," said Jim.

Mr. Harrison climbed the front steps. "With all due respect, Mrs. Dunbar," he said. "Your boy has grown to a man since your husband went to war. He can handle that horse."

Ma stood her ground. "I won't lose my son the day after burying my only brother."

Mr. Harrison walked back into the yard. "Saddle him up," he said to Jim. "I'll ride Buck to town if that's what it takes to prove he's broke."

Jim climbed to the top step. He was taller than Ma now, forcing her to look up to him. "Buck won't throw me," he said. "I trained him with respect, the way Pa taught me."

Ma's face softened. She turned to Simon's pa. "Do you believe he's thoroughly broken?"

"Indeed I do," said Mr. Harrison. "I've watched over his training since Alexander went to war. Jim has done a fine job. I'm certain he can ride without being tossed."

"All right," said Ma.

Jim let out a whoop. He took off running up the path before Ma could change her mind.

Ma sighed. "Is there any more news about Morgan's army?" she asked Mr. Harrison.

"That's why we're headed to town," said Simon. "To hear the latest."

"I want to go," said Dill.

Ma shook her head. "With your uncle's death and funeral, we're two days behind on the chores. I need your help with the washing." She turned to Simon. "There's a slice of peach pie for you, if you bring Jim back in one piece."

Simon rubbed his stomach. "Can I have a taste before we go?"

Ma pushed Simon's hair off his forehead. "Not 'til you return from town." She nodded at Dill. "Let's get to the washing."

Dill dragged her feet as she carried the pail to the rain barrel. The most exciting moment in Jackson County history and here she was, stuck on the farm. If only she had been born a boy, she would not have to stay behind to wash clothes.

Buck galloped into the yard with Jim on his back. The buckskin stallion pranced in the morning light making Dill wonder if Ma had made a mistake allowing Jim to ride. Ma must've been thinking the same thing. She shook her finger at Mr. Harrison. "So help me, Jeremiah. If that horse throws my son, I'll have your good name."

Mr. Harrison tipped his hat. "Understood."

Simon settled on the bench, beside his pa.

"Wait!" Dill shouted. She set the pail of rainwater on the front step. "I'm ready to choose my fabric now."

Ma put her hands on her hips. "Whatever are you talking about?"

"For my new dress," said Dill. "You offered to make me a new dress, for my birthday." Dill held out the skirt of her old, blue work dress. It was worn so thin in spots, the sunlight passed through. "If Mr. Harrison can drop me at Mr. Vaughn's store, I'll choose the fabric."

Simon smiled. "Can Dill come with us?" he asked his pa.

"Certainly," said Mr. Harrison.

Ma lifted Dill's chin to look into her eyes. "Something tells me you have other motivations."

"Please, Ma," said Dill. "I can ride in the wagon."

"You certainly won't ride on that horse."

"Then I can go?"

Ma looked at the Harrison's wagon. "Get your bonnet," she said. "Bring her straight home," she told Mr. Harrison, "so she can hang the clothes to dry."

Mr. Harrison nodded. "Yes, ma'am."

Dill hurried down the front steps carrying her bonnet. Simon had already climbed into the bed of the wagon to make room on the bench. Once Dill was settled, Mr. Harrison nodded to Jim. Buck took off like the start of a race.

Mr. Harrison snapped the reins. "Hold tight!" he shouted.

The horses jolted forward through the buckskin stallion's dust. Dill held tight to the bench. She was not about to fall out of the wagon and miss the most exciting day in the history of Jackson County.

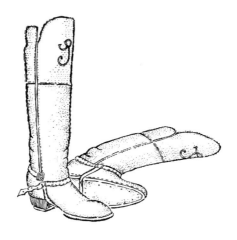

CHAPTER SIX

The Harrison's wagon raced past fields of shoulder-high corn. Jim's cornrows were crooked compared to their father's arrow-straight ones. Pa would've given Jim a talking-to if he'd been home. But then, Pa took a special pride in their farm.

All he had owned when he'd arrived from Scotland were the clothes on his back and his pap's rusty rabbit shooter. Pa couldn't believe his good fortune when he came to Jackson and was given this parcel of land to till. "In the shadow of Cemetery Hill," he always said.

Folks thought Alexander Dunbar was one peach shy of a full bushel, accepting the ghosts of Jackson's founding fathers as his neighbors. But Pa didn't give a lick about what other folks thought. These eighty acres were pure gold in his eyes. And he had turned them into gold through his hard work.

In 1862, Pa had left the farm to help President Lincoln defend the Union. If only he'd known the Rebels would raid on Ohio the following summer, he might never have left.

The closer the Harrison's wagon got to Jackson, the more crowded it became on the main road. Horses and riders passed on both sides of the wagon, making it take longer than usual to pass through the familiar streets. Jim was already standing in front of Vaughn's Mercantile when Mr. Harrison pulled his team up to the door.

Simon hopped down and offered his hand to Dill as if she were a proper lady. "Thank you for the ride," she said.

Mr. Vaughn stood in the door of his shop wearing a white apron and a big smile. "I've been waiting for you to come to town," he said to Jim. "I've got something for you." He led them past rows of hats, barrels of crackers and spools of twine. "Your pa wrote to me from Vicksburg," he said, reaching under a counter. "He thought you might be ready for these."

Jim gasped at the sight of the tall, black, riding boots. "You bet I'm ready," he said. He picked up a boot and held it to his foot. "How did you know my size?"

Mr. Vaughn winked. "They're the same size as the work boots your mother picked up last month. Try them on."

Jim unlaced his work boots and handed them to Dill. He slipped his feet into the riding boots. Dill slid her finger over a fancy letter "J" tooled in the black leather. "Look at this," she said.

"The J is for James," said Mr. Vaughn. He reached into his apron pocket and pulled out a piece of paper with their father's handwriting on it. "Ordered special, from your pa."

Jim took the paper from Mr. Vaughn. "Can I keep this?"

"Absolutely," said Mr. Vaughn. "Congratulations, son, on breaking that buckskin stallion." He turned to Dill. "What about you, young lady? Can I help you find something?"

Dill looked around the store. She'd almost forgotten why she'd come to town. "Ma wants to make me a dress for my birthday," she said, smiling. "I'm here to pick out the fabric."

Mr. Vaughn nodded. "Yes, indeed," he said. "A pretty young lady deserves a nice, new dress. Follow me."

Dill followed the shopkeeper to a back corner. "I just got in some new fabrics from Cincinnati," he said, leading Dill to a shelf filled with bolts of cloth. He pointed to a stool next to a closed door. "Stand on this if you need to reach anything on the higher shelves," he said. "Or ask your brother to get it for you. He must've grown a foot in the last two months."

Mr. Vaughn hurried off to tend to other customers. Jim stood before a mirror, admiring his new boots. "What do you think?" he asked. "Do I look like a soldier?"

Dill frowned. "That's not why Pa sent them to you." She tilted her head. Something was clicking on the other side of the door. "Do you hear that?" she asked.

Jim nodded. "It's coming from the telegraph office."

Dill pulled on the doorknob. Sure enough; the back of Mr. Vaughn's store connected to the telegraph office on Walnut Street. The messages coming across the wire gave the room the sound of meadow crickets on a summer evening. Dill could see Mr. Samuels bent over the telegraph machine, scribbling. Sheriff Selfridge leaned over the telegraph operator's shoulder, reading the words as he took them down.

The men filling up the telegraph office were dressed in every manner. Dill spotted Reverend Loxley in his preacher's collar on the far side of the counter. Behind him stood Mr. Landrum, his work clothes covered with dust. Mr. Harrison was squeezed into a corner with Simon. As Dill watched, Simon climbed on a chair and grabbed a rafter, pulling himself up to sit above the crowd with two other boys.

The telegraph stopped clicking long enough for Mr. Samuels to hand his paper to the sheriff. The men across the counter stopped talking.

"*Morgan's Raiders in Brown County,*" read the Sheriff.

"That's just three counties away!" shouted Mr. Landrum.

The Sheriff held up his hand for quiet. "*1,900 Rebels heading east. Robbing banks. Looting stores. Stealing horses. Hobson's Union Army more than six hours behind Morgan's cavalry.*"

Sheriff Selfridge slammed his fist on the counter. "Prepare for war!" he shouted. "Bury all that is valuable. Hide your horses. Meet back here tomorrow. Bring every able bodied man. It will take all of us to defend Jackson."

Dill felt a hand on her shoulder. Mr. Vaughn's white apron loomed over her. "That news was not for the ears of a young lady like you, Cordelia." He pulled a peppermint stick from his pocket and stuck it in her hand. "Hurry home, now, and help your mother hide your family's silver."

Jim stared into the telegraph office. "I s'pect I'm too late to join the governor's militia," he said.

"Sounds like the sheriff needs your help defending Jackson," said Mr. Vaughn. "Come back tomorrow."

Dill and Jim followed Mr. Vaughn to the front of the store. Simon and Mr. Harrison had already pulled the wagon up to the curb. "Get in," shouted Simon. "We've got to get back to our farms."

Dill's mind raced. She wondered how Ma would react to the news. As she reached for the rail of the wagon, Mr. Vaughn's peppermint stick slipped through her hand, landing in the dirt. Dill reached down to pick it up, but stopped. Not even the sweetest candy could remove the bitter taste of war.

CHAPTER SEVEN

Mr. Harrison drove his team out of Jackson even faster than they'd arrived. Jim raced ahead on Buck. His new boots were covered in dust stirred up by the other horses and wagons.

Nellie's howl rang out the moment they turned down the lane. The little beagle met them half way to the house. Ma stood in the yard, hanging the last towel up to dry.

"Wait 'til you hear," shouted Dill. "The Rebels are in Brown County."

Ma's eyes grew wide. "Isn't anyone going to stop them?"

Simon's pa shook his head. "The Union forces can't close the gap. Sheriff Selfridge sent us home to prepare for war."

Jim climbed down from Buck and wiped the dust off his riding boots.

"Where did you get those boots?" asked Ma.

Jim pulled Pa's letter from his pocket and gave it to his mother. Ma smiled. "That's just like your pa to think of your needs while neglecting his own."

Simon pointed to the fancy design in the leather. "They even have the letter J tooled in 'em."

"For James," said Dill.

"Did you pick out the material for your new dress?" asked Ma.

"Oh no," said Dill. "I forgot all about it."

Ma shook her head. "That was the reason you went to town."

"There was a lot of commotion in Jackson," said Mr. Harrison, stepping down from the wagon. "The sheriff is calling for a local militia." He nodded toward Jim. "He's going to need every hand he can get."

Ma's face turned red. "I didn't raise my son to become cannon fodder."

"I'll take Buck to the barn," said Jim. His jaw muscle was bulged out so far, you'd've thought he had a wad of tobacco in his cheek.

Simon climbed the front steps. "We brought Jim back in one piece," he said. "I want my pie."

Ma grabbed Dill by the arm. "Take Simon to the well, with a bar of soap," she whispered. "I don't want to see a speck of dirt on his hands when he sits down at the table."

Dill carried Jim's work boots through the parlor and set them by the back door. She picked up Ma's soap from the drying rack above the washbasin. "First one to the well gets the biggest slice of pie," she shouted to Simon.

Simon's bare feet pounded the path behind Dill. She lowered the bucket into the well and listened for the splash at the bottom. "Here," she said, shoving the soap into Simon's fist. "You'll need this to cut through the layers of dirt."

Simon pushed the soap back at Dill. "Pa says heaven welcomes those who're clean inside and out." He shook his head. "I ain't ready to die."

Dill looked into her friend's dirt-streaked face. "Is that why you won't take a bath, Simon? You think you'll die if you get too clean?"

Simon looked down at his filthy feet. He had turned eleven back in May, but right now he looked like a frightened little boy. Dill shoved the soap into his hands again. "Ma makes Jim and me take a bath every Saturday night. And we're not dead. Besides, she won't let you near our table with those filthy hands."

Simon took the soap. "I reckon it wouldn't hurt to wash my hands."

Dill poured water from the bucket. The white soap turned brown as Simon turned it over and over in his hands. It took three buckets of water, but at last, his pink skin showed through. He dried his hands on his shirt, leaving two gray smudges. "Let's eat," he said.

Dill trotted a little slower back to the house so Simon could get to the kitchen first. He slid into a chair next to Jim. Mr. Harrison smiled at his son's clean hands as Ma set a slice of pie in front of him. Simon licked the peach filling before digging into the crust with his fork.

Mr. Harrison stirred two lumps of sugar into his coffee and took a sip. "I've brought your ma up-to-date on the news from town," he said. He stuck his fork into his pie and brought a bite to his lips.

Ma's cheeks were still red from doing the wash in the afternoon sun. "Sounds like they're crossing Ohio faster than anyone expected."

"Our Union army can't catch 'em," said Jim.

Ma gasped. "When will the governor's militia get here?"

"Not soon enough," said Simon's pa. He washed a bite of pie down with coffee. "At this pace, Morgan and his men will be in Jasper by tomorrow afternoon."

"That's just west of Piketon," said Ma.

Simon raised his empty plate. Ma shook her head. "Don't want to spoil your supper."

"We won't have an evening meal unless Pa can shoot us a rabbit," said Simon.

Dill looked at Simon's skinny arms. More than likely, her mother's pie would be the only meal he'd eat that day.

Ma set another slice of pie on Simon's plate. He gobbled it down in three bites, then turned to Dill. "Let's go see Buck."

Jim picked up his plate and carried it to the washbasin.

Ma poured more coffee for Mr. Harrison, but set her own cup in the washbasin. "The hot sun wore me out." She pushed a lock of hair off her forehead. "I think I'll lie down for a spell."

"Of course," said Mr. Harrison. "Do you mind if I finish my coffee on the porch, with Jim?"

Ma nodded. "Please stay and visit." She turned to Dill. "Will you take the washtubs to the cellar?"

"Yes ma'am," said Dill. She picked up a leftover biscuit and slipped it into Simon's pocket on their way out the door.

CHAPTER EIGHT

Outside the kitchen, the afternoon sun beat down on the farm. Locusts buzzed in the walnut tree. Everything felt so ordinary. It was hard to believe Rebels were three counties west of Jackson.

"What's the matter with your ma?" asked Simon.

"I don't know." Dill shrugged. "Can you help me carry these washtubs to our cellar?"

Simon shook his head. "I'm going to look for a place to hide Buck," he said. "Meet me at his pen."

Dill frowned. "Don't you think of riding him."

Simon pulled the biscuit from his pocket and bit off half. "I ain't promising nothing," he said.

Dill dragged the washtubs behind the buggy shed to where her pa had dug a cellar into the hillside before she was born. Pa had designed the heavy wooden doors to stay shut through the full force of a Midwestern tornado. It took all of

Dill's strength to open them. She dragged the washtubs through the doorway and down two short steps, stopping on the bottom step to let her eyes adjust to the dim light. A long earthen hallway led to a hollowed-out cellar that stayed the same temperature year round.

Ma's pickles and fruit preserves filled up ceramic crocks on wooden shelves across one side of the cellar. Dusty cobwebs stretched from the lower shelves to the upper ones. Off to one side, a dark chunk of polished wood leaned against a stack of empty crocks. Dill stepped around the washtubs to get a closer look. The barrel of a gun connected to the polished wooden handle. The gun's long barrel leaned against the wall.

So this was where Pa had left his pap's Scottish rabbit shooter.

Dill brushed the cobwebs from the barrel and lifted the wooden stock off the floor. The gun's cold steel tingled in her hand.

The old flintlock was heavier than the shotgun Pa had taken to war. Longer, too. It took all her strength to raise the stock to her shoulder. Dill shut one eye and gazed down the long barrel, pointing it up the steps toward the daylight. With a load of powder and lead, this gun could help her protect the farm. Dill searched for the lock with her thumb and pulled it all the way back. It took two fingers to squeeze the trigger. *Click!*

A shadowy shape stood in the doorway. Nellie shook her spotted coat and settled back in the dirt.

Dill's heart felt like it might leap from her chest. Thank goodness the gun had not been loaded. She leaned the barrel against the wall and rushed through the narrow corridor. When she reached the door, she knelt down and stuck her nose in the ruff of Nellie's back. The beagle thumped her tail in the dirt.

The thought of someone shooting Nellie made Dill's chest ache. She raced back to the cellar and pulled Grandpap's musket to her chest. She would shoot any Rebel who threatened to harm Nellie or Buck, or even Ol' Luke. This was her farm. Rebels were not welcome here.

CHAPTER NINE

Dill held tight to her grandpap's musket. With each step closer to the barn, she felt stronger. She had no gunpowder or lead balls to shove down the barrel, but she would get her hands on both before the Rebels raided Jackson.

Nellie was the first to reach Buck's pen. Simon stood on the top rail holding out a fistful of grass. The beagle's howl surprised him. He dropped to his seat, grabbing the split rail to keep from falling. "Darn dog," he shouted. "Another second and I'd've been on Buck's back."

Dill trotted up to the fence. She let the barrel of Grandpap's musket slide through her hand until the wooden stock touched the dirt.

Simon swung his legs over the fence. "That's an old flintlock, ain't it? Let me hold it," he said, taking the gun from Dill. He shut one eye and peered down the barrel toward the house. "It's not loaded, is it?"

Dill stroked Nellie's spotted back. "Not yet."

Simon pulled the lock back with his thumb. "This gun must be a hundred years old. Does it still fire?"

"It will," said Dill, "when there's a load in it."

Simon squeezed the trigger. The lock slammed closed. *Click!* A grin spread across his lips. "You're going to fight the Rebels with this gun, aren't you?" Dill's nod made Simon laugh. "You couldn't hit the side of a barn with this old thing."

"Yes, I could," said Dill. "It's my Scottish grandpap's rabbit shooter."

"I don't know about Scottish rabbits, but the critters on this side of the ocean would fall down laughing at a man trying to catch his supper with this rusty musket."

Dill took the rabbit shooter back from Simon. "The sight of it will scare those Rebels," she said lifting the gun to her chest. "The barrel must be four feet long."

"Is that how you judge a gun? By the length of its barrel?"

Dill's face felt hot. "It looks scary to me."

Simon scowled. "Let me tell you what's scary," he said. "Two thousand Rebels riding into Jackson. They won't line up all friendly-like at the Isham House Inn, waiting for their supper. No sir. They'll fan out across this county, stealing every ounce of bacon from every smokehouse."

Dill ran her hand down the gun's smooth barrel. "Do you think they'll make it to Jackson, Simon?"

"I know they will," said Simon. "And we'd better be ready." He picked up a rock and hurled it at the side of the barn. The rock hit the wooden slats with a *bang*. "Sheriff Selfridge told my pa about the heartache the Rebels've caused folks across Indiana. I'll tell you, if you want to know."

Dill stared at the spot where the rock had hit. "Speak on it," she said.

"They're burnin' down farms."

Dill wrapped her braids around her fingers. "What are they burning? Sheds? Barns? Houses?"

"All of those things. And more. They're chasing folks off, stealing everything that ain't nailed down. Burning the rest to the ground."

Dill looked down the hill at the house her pa had built with his own two hands. The thought of it going up in flames made her head hurt. "I wish this war had never been started," she said.

"Too late for that. The war's not only started, it's coming our way." Simon nodded at the gun in her hand. "And no farm girl with her grandpap's rusty musket is going to stop it."

Dill leaned the flintlock against the rails of Buck's pen. It didn't look scary any more. It looked old and useless. "What do we do?"

"What everyone else is doing," said Simon. "Find a place to hide your valuables," he nodded in Buck's direction. "Especially him."

Dill climbed over the split rails and rubbed Buck's warm muzzle. "Help me think of a place."

Simon looked around the Dunbar farm. "How about the buggy shed?"

"They're burning down sheds. You said so yourself."

"You're right. You can't hide him in the barn either. What about the house?"

The thought of Buck hiding in Ma's parlor made Dill laugh. "Not the house," she said. "Ma would throw a fit at the mess he'd make."

"It's got to be someplace dark and quiet," said Simon.

"I know," said Dill. "C'mon." She trotted to the far end of Buck's pen, opening the gate for Simon then closing it fast. Buck pounded his hoof. He'd gotten a taste of running earlier that day and wanted more.

Dill climbed the gate and rubbed Buck's soft muzzle. "Stay here," she said. "For now."

Nellie led the way down the hill, past row after row of corn. At the split rail fence, she veered left and trotted down a steep trail. "This way," Dill called to Simon.

A raccoon dashed out of the thicket, disappearing into the shadows. The dirt turned cold under their feet. "I know where you're going," said Simon. "The cave spring."

"Yes," said Dill. The cave spring was as familiar to her as any room in her house. Years ago, Pa had built a springhouse over the stream that flowed from the cave into Salt Lick Creek. The cool water kept their butter and milk fresh, even in the hottest months. The hollow surrounding the cave was not visible from the barn, making it the perfect hiding place.

The willows closed in as they reached the mouth of the cave. Dragonflies fluttered above the pool. A bullfrog croaked before leaping into the water, sending rings across the smooth surface. Dill dipped a toe in the pool. The cold water sent a chill up her spine.

Simon splashed through the pool to the mouth of the cave. He bumped his head against the smooth, rock ceiling. "Buck'll never fit in here," he said, his voice echoing back from the dark hole.

"I know," said Dill. "But we can hide him in this hollow."

"What if he wanders off?"

"We'll tie him to a willow tree."

Simon shook the trunk of a small willow. "You're right. This is a good hiding spot." He looked up the streambed toward the entrance to the hollow. "Buck's hooves will leave footprints in the mud."

"We can fix that," said Dill. She reached her hand out to Simon. "Give me your jackknife."

Simon pulled his knife from his pocket. "Here," he said, opening the blade.

Dill hacked off a willow branch "Use this to scrape the mud."

Simon swept the willow switch across the mud, covering all signs they'd been there. When they reached the cornfield, a whistle pierced the air. Nellie barked.

"It's my pa," said Simon. "I'll race you."

Dill raced Simon up the hill and down the path to the house. Mr. Harrison stood on the front steps saying good-bye to Ma and Jim. Simon poked Dill in the side. "Better hide your grandpap's old flintlock," he said. "Don't want to scare any Scottish rabbits."

Dill hurried back to Buck's pen. She carried the old flintlock into the barn and hauled it up the ladder, laying it lengthwise on a beam beside the loft window. Their house looked naked on its knoll beside the buggy shed. Dill ran a hand down the barrel of Grandpap's gun. From this vantage point she could take on a whole army of Rebels.

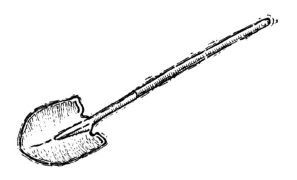

CHAPTER TEN

Dill woke the next morning to the sound of coughing. Not one little cough, but a long, drawn-out wheeze.

In the kitchen, Jim was slapping their mother's back so hard, you'd've thought she was a mule refusing to plow. When she finally stopped coughing, she stayed bent over the hearth, her hand to her throat.

"Are you all right?" Dill asked.

Ma sat back on her stool. Her face looked redder than the day before. "I woke with a tickle in my throat," she whispered. "And I can't stop coughing."

Dill laid the back of her hand against her mother's forehead like Ma always did when she or Jim were sick. "You're hot as a flat iron," said Dill.

"Shall I fetch Doc Miller?" asked Jim.

Ma shook her head. "There's no time for that." She flipped the egg she'd been frying in the skillet. "We have to bury our valuables."

Dill noticed a folded piece of white cloth draped over the back of her chair. "Shall I put our silver in here?" she asked, unfolding an old pillowcase.

Jim spread honey on a square of cornbread. "Yep," he said. "I'll go dig a hole in the orchard while you and Ma collect everything."

Ma put the egg on a plate and carried it to the table. She took two steps back toward the fire before bending over to cough again. When she stood back up, her face was pale as a sheet. Jim jumped to his feet in time to catch her as she slumped to the floor.

Dill's eyes grew wide. "What's wrong with her?"

"I don't know," said Jim. "Help me get her into bed. I'll ride to town for Doc Miller."

Once Ma was in bed, the color came back to her face. She opened her eyes. Her voice came out in a whisper. "Don't worry about the doctor. Bury the silver," she said. "Men at war become half animal. They'll steal anything they can lay their hands on." She looked at Jim. "Don't forget your father's watch."

Jim nodded. He sat down at the table and pulled on his new boots before hurrying out the kitchen door.

Dill ate a bite of cornbread. She poked her fork into her fried egg. Yellow goo from the egg oozed onto her plate, taking away her appetite. She scraped her breakfast into the scrap pail and snatched the pillowcase off her chair.

To see the parlor, you'd've thought Ma was expecting her quilting group. There was not a speck of dust on anything. Her silver candlesticks shone from their spot on the table. Dill picked up the candlesticks and dropped them into the pillowcase. They made a clanking sound at the bottom.

Grandma's clock chimed from its spot over the fireplace. The old wood and glass clock had kept time on the mantel ever since Dill could remember. She set the pillowcase on the floor and lifted the clock off its perch. A chiming clock could not be buried with the rest of their valuables. The sound would give away their hiding spot.

Dill carried the clock across the hall and opened her parents' bureau. Pa's side was empty, except for a woolen blanket. She wrapped the clock in the blanket and set it in the back, on Pa's side. She tried not to think of how the bureau would go up in flames if the Rebels set fire to the house.

A faded likeness of Dill's Wellington grandparents stood in its silver frame on Ma's wooden chest. Her grandmother had always looked so stern in this image. Nothing like the grandma they'd visited in Pennsylvania the summer before last. Dill laid the portrait in the pillowcase, silver frame and all.

Ma watched from her bed. "Don't forget the likeness of our family," she whispered.

Another frame on her mother's chest held a portrait of their family taken three years ago, when Dill was nearly eight.

They had dressed in their Sunday best to pose for a traveling artist. Pa's face was frozen in that half smile he always wore when he was playing tricks on Ma. Dill smiled back at Pa before laying his likeness right side up so as not to cover his grin.

There were a few more things to collect: Ma's necklace with the silver locket, the platter trimmed in gold that had been a wedding gift to Ma and Pa, a comb with a silver strip along the back side. Dill stopped to admire each item before putting it in the sack. Finally, when the house seemed bare, she lifted the pillowcase over her shoulder and stepped out the back door.

The orchard lay across the north pasture, on the banks of Salt Lick Creek. She could see Jim from the shoulders up, shoveling dirt into a pile. As she approached, she noticed an enormous book laying beside the hole. Seeing it there made Dill's load feel twice as heavy. "Do we have to bury the Dunbar Bible?" she asked as she stepped around the dirt pile.

Jim nodded. "Ma's orders."

Dill set the pillowcase on the ground. "Can I see our names before it goes in the sack?" Jim climbed out of the hole and flipped the Bible to the middle pages. Dill ran her finger over Pa's name and birth date, Ma and Pa's wedding date, and the wedding date of her Dunbar grandparents. Her full name and birthday were there, too, in Pa's neat handwriting, along with Jim's.

Jim closed the Bible. He sifted through the contents of the sack and nodded his approval. A crow peered down from the apple tree, cocking its head as if inspecting the family silver. *"Caw!"* it said.

"What about Pa's watch?" asked Dill.

Jim turned and stared across Salt Lick Creek.

Dill shook the sack. The family silver jangled at the bottom.

Jim folded his arms across his chest. "It's like burying a piece of him."

The crow cawed, louder this time, as if telling Jim to drop in the watch. Jim grabbed a clump of dirt and hurled it at the crow. The clump smacked the tree branch, raining dirt into the pillowcase. The big bird beat its wings against the air. *"Caw! Caw! Caw!"* it nagged as it flew across the pasture.

Jim spat into the dirt pile. Dill gasped. Spitting was a behavior their mother never tolerated.

Finally Jim reached into his pocket and pulled out Pa's gold watch. He flicked his thumb on the button, opening the lid. Dill stood on her toes to look into the watch's ivory face. Twelve gold hatch marks glittered in the morning sun. Jim wound the stem. He closed his eyes and held the watch to his ear.

"Can I listen?" asked Dill.

Jim took his time unhooking the gold chain from his belt loop. He held the watch to Dill's ear. The tiny *tick, tick, tick* made her smile.

Jim snapped the lid shut. He slipped the watch into its doeskin pouch and laid it in the pillowcase. "There," he said.

He pulled a piece of twine from his pocket and wrapped it around the top of the pillowcase.

Dill squatted down to set the sack in the hole. The pillowcase looked pale against the brown dirt. Without saying a word, Dill took the shovel and scooped dirt over the pillowcase. The hole was half-way filled when Jim took over shoveling. In no time, the dirt was back in the ground where it belonged. He stepped on the loose dirt to flatten it.

Dill picked up a tree branch and tossed it on the bare patch. "The fresh dirt will tell them something's buried here," she said. "We have to cover it."

She dragged sticks and branches from around the orchard, covering the ground under the tree. Soon there was no sign of the family's buried treasure.

Jim lifted the shovel to his shoulder and lit out across the pasture. Dill trotted after him. "I hate those Rebels," she said when she'd caught up.

Jim bit his lower lip.

"What about you?" asked Dill. "Don't you hate 'em, too?"

The tool shed door stood open. "Truth be known," Jim said, hanging the shovel between two pegs, "when this war began, I hated every Rebel and every Rebel's kin." He closed the door and hurried toward the barn. Dill ran to keep up.

Jim opened the barn door. "I hated 'em for starting this war. For taking Pa away from us," he said, reaching for Buck's bridle.

Dill climbed up to sit on the edge of Buck's stall. "Don't you hate 'em even more, now that they're raiding on Ohio?"

Jim stuck the bit in Buck's mouth and reached for his saddle. When he had the saddle buckled on Buck's back, he looked into Dill's face. "One night last spring, I couldn't sleep for all the hate welling up inside of me. I thought of something Pa had told me, a few years back, when I'd picked a fight at school."

"What was that?" asked Dill.

Jim picked up Buck's brush and slid it down the horse's broad flank. His strokes were long and gentle. "Pa said hate don't do a lick of harm to the other man," he said. "But it can shrivel the heart of the fellow doing the hating. It can make his heart so small, there's nothing left to beat."

Dill stuck her hand under her pinafore. The thumping in her chest felt steady as ever. "Does your heart ever ache for missing Pa?" she asked.

Jim cinched down the saddle straps. "Not so much any more," he said. "But in the first months he was gone, it ached a bundle. I felt certain he'd come home in a pinewood box." He patted Buck's tan muzzle. "Pa's gold watch held me together."

Dill waited for her brother to explain how a pocket watch could hold a body together. "What about Pa's watch?" she finally asked.

Jim looked out the barn door. "Nights were the worst," he said. "I'd get to thinking about Pa camped on the edge of some battlefield. I'd hold his watch to my ear until I fell asleep. I figured if Pa's gold watch was still ticking, it meant his heart was still beating."

A lump filled Dill's throat. She jumped off the rail and wrapped her arms around her brother's middle. "I'm sorry I made you bury it," she said. "Let's go dig it up."

Jim rested his cheek on top of Dill's head. "No," he said. "It's safer buried in the orchard."

Dill hugged her brother as hard as she used to hug their pa. "Why did he have to go to war, Jim?"

Jim lifted his cheek from Dill's head. "What do you mean?"

"He's so much older than the other soldiers. Seems like he could've stayed home instead of signing up to fight."

Jim shook his head. "That would never have worked for Pa. He believes every man deserves a chance to work hard and raise a family. Even the colored man."

Dill thought of the dark skinned family living up Salt Lick Hollow. They had a girl named Dora who was about her age. "Is that why Pa is fighting? For colored men and their families?"

Jim took a handful of oats and held them up for Buck to nibble. "Pa told me he joined the Union army because the Southern folks' slaves deserve to be free."

"He'll come home," said Dill. "I know he will."

Jim wiped his sleeve across his face and picked up a pail. "Shall I milk Sadie before I fetch Doc Miller?"

"I'll do it," said Dill. "But I want to show you something first.

Dill ran the length of the barn and climbed to the loft. She lowered Grandpap's musket and carried it to Buck's stall. "We have to protect the farm," she said. "For Pa." She reached the gun out to Jim. "Help me load it."

Jim's mouth fell open. "What in the devil's name?"

"It's Grandpap's rabbit shooter."

"I know what it is. Where did you find it?"

"In the cellar, next to Ma's pickles and preserves," said Dill.

Jim lifted the gun to his cheek and looked down the barrel. "Well, I'll be a wet hen. I didn't know Pa had kept this old thing."

Dill grinned up at Jim. "When you go to town to fetch Doc Miller, pick up some gunpowder and lead balls."

Jim rested the gun's wooden stock on his boot. "I don't like the way you're thinking," he said. "You can't go shooting folks, not even Rebels."

"Why not?" asked Dill. "They're evil, ain't they?"

Jim shook his head. "Have you ever killed anything bigger than a spider?"

Dill's smile turned to a frown. "What's that got to do with shooting Rebels?"

"The first time I shot a rabbit, it screamed like a little girl. It was three weeks before I got the sound out of my head." Jim leaned the gun against the side of Buck's stall. "And another thing," he added. "You can't protect the farm with this old gun. Not when the Rebels are shooting Miniés. You'll get yourself killed." He picked up the milk pail and handed it to Dill. "Put the gun back where you found it," he said. "Milk Sadie while I ride to town for Doc Miller."

Dill hauled Grandpap's rusty musket back to the hayloft. From the window she could see Ol' Luke scratching himself against the fencepost Pa had replaced before riding off to war. In the distance, the chickens hunted grubs around the hen house Pa had whitewashed in his last weekend at home. Her pa's hard work was visible in every corner of their farm, from the split rails in the fence to the shingles on the roof of the house.

Dill laid Grandpap's gun on the beam. If Jim wouldn't shoot at the Rebels, it would be up to her to protect the farm. She would not let Pa return to find his home burned to the ground.

CHAPTER ELEVEN

Jim had just climbed into the saddle when an urgent howl rang out from the front porch. It was the kind of baying Nellie reserved for a fox circling the hen house.

Dill stopped milking and ran from the barn to see who it was. Simon Harrison drove his father's champion horses up their lane. His hair blew back as the team stormed into the yard. He pulled back on the reins just in time to keep the team from crashing into the porch rail.

Nellie circled the Harrison's wagon, howling so loud you'd've thought the house was on fire.

"Shush," Dill called to the beagle.

Nellie stopped long enough to sniff the air, then went back to howling.

Simon's blond hair lay loose on top of his head. A pink color filled his cheeks. "Why Simon," said Dill. "I believe you've had a bath."

Simon hopped off the wagon and reached a hand out to Nellie. You'd've thought she was meeting a porcupine. She held her ears flat against her head. The ruff of her neck stood up. She sniffed the front and back of Simon's hand before wagging the tip of her tail.

Dill laughed. "She doesn't recognize you without your stink."

Simon's neck turned red. The color crawled up his face, filling his cheeks. "After washing my hands, I figured your Ma's pie was my last earthly meal. But when I woke up on this side of the grass I figured I might as well clean my whole self."

"How many tubs of water did it take to get you clean?" asked Dill.

Simon grinned. "Pa claimed the well went dry. But he didn't care." He tugged at his shirt. "He gave me some new clothes."

Sure enough; Simon had on a new, white shirt. "You cleaned up real nice," said Dill.

"Thank you," said Simon.

Jim rode Buck into the yard. "Where's your pa?" he asked.

The smile vanished from Simon's face. "Sheriff Selfridge sent me," he said. "He wants your help dropping trees across the road from Piketon."

Jim's eyes grew wide. "Are they in Jackson County?"

"They're close," said Simon. "Pa's been patrolling the county line since dawn. He startled two of Morgan's advance guards at the border."

Jim's face turned white. "Shall I bring our old musket?"

"No," said Simon. "Bring your ax. Leave Buck behind, so they don't steal him."

Jim shot a glance to Dill before turning Buck to the barn.

"Have you had a meal today?" asked Dill.

Simon shook his head. His face looked thinner without all the layers of dirt. Dill led him through the front parlor. "Where's your ma?" he asked, looking around.

"She's not feeling well, so she's lying down," said Dill.

Simon peered down the hall. "Can I tell her the news?"

"I don't reckon it will hurt," said Dill, nodding to her mother's room.

Ma looked limp as a dishrag in her bed. Her normally strong voice came out in a whisper. "Where's your pa?"

"He's patrolling the county line with the sheriff," Simon whispered back. "Morgan's in Pike County."

Ma's eyes grew big as saucers. At that moment, a coughing fit made her stop talking and hold her ribs. Dill dipped a rag in the basin and laid it on her mother's forehead.

In the kitchen, Simon pulled a chair up to the table. "Your ma doesn't look so good."

"I know," said Dill. "She almost fainted at breakfast. Jim was going to get Doc Miller when you showed up."

The kitchen door flew open. Jim leaned the handle of an ax against the table and pulled up a chair. "I'm not wearing my new boots to chop down trees," he said. He pulled off his riding boots and laced up his work boots.

Dill set a plate in front of Simon. "What about Ma?" she asked Jim. "She needs a doctor."

Simon looked up from his plate. "I can bring Doc Miller back with me," he said, "before I go home to defend our farm."

Jim stood by the door. "Who's going to protect our farm if I leave?" he asked.

Dill stood up. "I will," she said. "Get me some gunpowder and lead."

"No," said Jim. He lifted the ax to his shoulder. "I'll help in town and be home before the Rebels get here."

"What about Buck?" asked Dill.

Jim stopped. "I had planned to ride him to town."

Simon pointed his fork at Dill. "Tell him about our hiding place."

"Simon and I found a spot to tie him up. It's in the hollow, by the cave spring," she said. "The Rebels will never find him down there."

Jim wiped his forehead with the collar of his shirt. "All right," he said. "If I'm not back by sunset, take him down there." He pulled on his hat. "C'mon Simon," he called from the parlor. "Let's go."

Dill followed Simon to the front door. "Get me a bag of lead balls," she whispered. "And some gunpowder."

Simon tipped his hat as if to say "all right". Jim leapt the gap between the porch and the wagon. Simon shook the reins and the horses took off at a gallop. Jim held tight to his hat. He didn't even turn to wave good-bye.

CHAPTER TWELVE

Dill washed and dried the dishes. She swept up the crumbs and laid the fire for supper. She scrubbed the kitchen floor, though it wasn't the least bit dirty.

The towels and bed sheets still hung on the clothesline from wash day. Dill took a stool to the back yard and unhooked the clothes pegs. She carried in the laundry, folded the sheets as neatly as she could, and tucked them all in the hall closet.

She walked into her mother's room, making sure not to step on the squeaky floorboard. Ma's face was redder than a pickled beet. Her breath came loud and raspy. A blue jay squawked in the walnut tree outside the window. Ma's eyelids didn't even flutter.

Dill touched her mother's face. The wet rag on her forehead could have come from the washtub, it was so hot. She dipped it in the basin and wrung it out before returning it to Ma's forehead.

Four muffled chimes sounded from the clock in the bureau. Two hours had passed since Jim had ridden off in the Harrisons' wagon. Simon should've been back with Doc Miller by now. What if Rebels had captured them?

Dill dropped onto the stool beside Ma's dressing table. The curtains hung loose around her open window. Above the meadow, a pair of butterflies fluttered in a delicate dance. Dill's heart raced. She could never tell her mother that Jim was a Rebel prisoner. Or worse, that he was dead.

Ma's mending basket sat on the floor beneath the window. Dill picked up one of Jim's shirts. Mending the hole in his sleeve would drive thoughts of Rebels from her mind. She clipped a long thread from a wooden spool and pulled a needle from the pincushion. No matter how she tried, the thread went above and below the needle, refusing to pass through its eye. She tossed the shirt back in the basket.

The clock chimed half past four. Ma kept sleeping. On any other day, she would be calling Dill to collect the eggs.

Dill rose and hurried through the kitchen, stopping to grab the egg basket. Nellie stretched in her spot beside the rain barrel before leading the way up the path.

The quiet of the hen house calmed Dill's nerves. There, with the soft clucking of the hens, she could almost believe Rebels weren't burning down farms in the next county. She stuck her hand into a nest. The hen flapped her wings and flew up to the rafters. She moved slower at the next nest. The hen squawked and flapped away. Dill could not hide her nervousness, even from the chickens. She filled her basket with eggs and hurried to the cellar.

Three days had passed since Jim had delivered eggs to Mr. Vaughn. Two full baskets awaited delivery. She set the third basket beside the others. The cool of the cellar would keep the eggs fresh until life returned to normal, if it ever returned to normal.

Nellie's howl rang out from the house. Dill hurried past the buggy shed in time to see Doc Miller draw his wagon up beside the front porch. Simon hopped to the ground. "Wait 'til you hear," he yelled. "The Rebels have crested Pike Hill."

Dill looked up at Doc Miller. "Is it true?"

The town's doctor nodded. His hair was grayer around the temples than Dill remembered, his face more wrinkled. He took Dill's hand and patted it gently. "Sorry to hear about your mother," he said. "Terrible timing, with Morgan's Raiders in the next county."

Dill looked up the lane. "Where's Jim?"

"Your brother joined the town's men. They're in the square, awaiting instructions from the sheriff," Doc said. He lifted a black bag from the wagon. "Show me to your mother."

As she led Doc through the parlor, Dill half expected to see Ma in the kitchen, making coffee. But when they rounded the parlor door, her heart sank. Ma hadn't moved in the hour since she had left her side. "Doc Miller is here," said Dill. She gave her mother's shoulder a gentle shake.

Ma blinked. "Thank goodness," she whispered.

Doc carried the washbasin to the window and dumped out the water. "Fill this with fresh water," he said, handing the basin to Dill. "The colder the better."

"The coldest water comes from our spring," said Dill. "It's in the hollow, behind the barn."

"Water from the well is fine for now," said Doc. "You can go to the spring after I leave."

Simon ran ahead of Dill. He dropped the bucket down the well. "Sorry it took me so long to get back," he said, pulling on the rope.

"You had me worried," said Dill. "Where were you?"

"At the telegraph office," said Simon. "You've never seen such a crowd."

"Bigger than yesterday?"

Simon nodded. "Everyone wants to know where the Rebels are headed next," he said. "Ol' Morgan ain't making it easy. He sent fake orders to his men in Chillicothe and Portsmouth, telling them to head south, across the Ohio River. The governor ordered gunboats to patrol the river. And all the while, the Rebels kept riding east. They're on the road from Beavertown now. Headed straight for Jackson."

Dill gasped. "What's to become of us?"

"The sheriff was fixing to lead the town's men out the Beavertown Road when we left town," said Simon. "Pa kept our horse team to haul logs. If they can drop enough trees across the Rebels' path, the governor's militia just might catch up to them."

Simon lifted the bucket from the well. "I brought you some gunpowder and lead," he said. "They're in Doc's wagon."

Dill thought about what Jim had said. Her stomach squeezed to a knot. "I've never fired a flintlock," she said. "I don't even know how to load one."

Simon poured water into the washbasin. "I'll show after Doc leaves."

Doc was stepping out of Ma's room by the time Dill returned with fresh water. His long mustache drooped, making his face look like he was frowning. He took off his glasses and cleaned the lenses with his handkerchief. The lines between his eyes were deeper than when he'd arrived. "I know your pa is at war," he said to Dill. "And your brother is in town. Do you have any other kin in Jackson?"

"She had an uncle," said Simon. "But he's dead. Shot in the belly by a Rebel."

Doc laid a hand on Dill's shoulder. "I was sorry to hear about Swinge."

"Thank you," said Dill.

Doc put on his glasses and adjusted them behind his ears. "Do you have anyone else? An uncle or aunt?"

Dill shook her head.

Doc stroked his mustache. "How old are you, Cordelia?"

"I'll be eleven next month," said Dill. She stood as straight and tall as she could.

Doc leaned against the fireplace. "What do you know about diphtheria?"

"Not diphtheria," gasped Simon. "That's what choked my ma."

Doc opened the front door. "Let's not scare Cordelia," he said, pushing Simon outside. Doc turned back to face Dill. "His mother's was the worst case of diphtheria I've ever seen," he said, pulling up a chair. "Your mother is strong. She'll pull through this, if you can keep her fever down. A cool rag on her forehead will help. Freshen it as often as you can with cold water. She's got a miserable sore throat, too. And it's only going to get worse. A wool scarf around her neck will comfort her." Doc looked out the window. "Honestly, Cordelia," he said. "We've got bigger worries. The whole town is set for war."

Dill felt her chest tighten. "Why did Ma have to come down with diphtheria now?"

"Don't you worry about the Rebels," said Doc. He touched Dill's cheek. His fingers felt rough and scratchy. "Just take care of your mother. Don't let her out of bed. And keep her cool. Do you think you can do that?"

Dill nodded. "I s'pect so."

Doc stepped out to the porch. "Help Cordelia," he said to Simon. "And don't cause any trouble." He climbed into his wagon and rattled down the lane.

Dill felt like crawling into bed and pulling the covers over her head. If only Jim hadn't been called to town. And Simon wasn't much help. Through the window she could see him sitting on the bench staring up at Cemetery Hill. She dragged herself out the front door. "Help me collect some water from the cave spring," she said.

Simon wiped his eyes with the back of his hand. "I got the gunpowder and lead from Doc's wagon. Shall we load your old flintlock?"

"Let's get the spring water first," said Dill. "We can hide Buck while we're at it."

A grin spread across Simon's face. "I'll ride him to the cave spring."

CHAPTER THIRTEEN

Dill stopped by the well to collect the pail while Simon kept running. "I told you I'd get the first ride," he called over his shoulder.

"It won't be a real ride," said Dill, hurrying to catch up. She opened the barn door and ran to Buck's pen. The feedbag hung from the nail where Jim always left it. Dill dropped a handful of oats into her pocket. She would need them to urge Buck down the muddy trail to the cave spring. He snorted as Dill slipped the halter over his head.

Simon swung a leg over Buck's broad back. The stallion stamped a hoof and whinnied. Dill offered up some oats. His soft muzzle tickled her palm. "You carry the pail," she said, handing Simon the bucket.

Simon took the handle with one hand. He held tight to Buck's mane with the other. The moment Dill opened the gate, he kicked his heels into the stallion's belly. Buck jerked hard against the lead rope.

"Stop that," Dill shouted. "We'll never get him into the hollow with you spooking him."

Simon frowned. "C'mon," he said. "Just give me one gallop around the meadow. I'll come right back. I promise."

"No," said Dill. "We've got to hide him so I can get back to Ma."

Dill led Buck past the cornfield and down the narrow path. She urged him through the deep mud to the rocky ground on the far side of the spring pool. "We'll tie him here," she said at last. "So his feet stay dry."

Simon slid to the ground. "That wasn't much of a ride."

"It'll have to do," said Dill. She tied Buck's lead to a willow trunk.

Buck pulled against the rope, testing Dill's knot. He stomped the rocky ground. Dill offered up the last of the oats. He pushed his muzzle into her palm. "We'll be back when it's safe for you," she said, kissing his soft nose.

Simon cut a willow branch and scraped the ground as they backed out of the hollow. He applied extra effort to cover Buck's deep hoof prints. By the time he had finished, there was no sign they'd been there.

At the barn, Dill lowered the old musket from its beam and handed it to Simon. "Show me how to shoot it."

Simon examined the gun's long barrel. "It's a bit rusty. But it should fire just fine."

He bit the end off a paper cone and poured gunpowder down the muzzle. Next he dropped down the lead ball and wadding and rammed them down the barrel with a long rod. "See the water gourd on the fence post across the yard?" Simon asked, pointing the gun's barrel out the barn door.

Dill nodded.

Blam!

The gourd dropped to the ground.

Dill's mouth fell open. In all the years she'd helped Simon with reading and sums, she'd never thought he was good at anything.

"Now you try it," he said, handing the musket to Dill.

Dill's fingers fumbled with the paper cone. She spilled gunpowder on the ground. "This is harder that it looks," she said, stuffing wadding down the barrel. She rested the gun's long barrel on the rail of Buck's pen. "What should I shoot?"

"Pick a target," said Simon. "Something close enough to hit."

Jim's straw hat, hung on a nail under the eaves of the tool shed. Dill closed one eye and aimed.

Blam!

She opened her eye. The hat had not moved.

"Did I even hit the tool shed?" she asked.

Simon shook his head. "Nobody hits their target on the first try."

He loaded the gun and aimed.

Blam!

Jim's hat spun and fell to the ground.

A smile spread across Dill's face. "You're a good shot," she said.

Simon puffed up like a rooster about to crow. "I get a lot of practice, helping my pa hunt."

"I never knew," said Dill, picking up the pail of water. "I need to get back to Ma. Will you reload the musket and set it on the rail in the loft?"

Simon lifted the flintlock. "All right," he said.

Dill was half way to the house when she heard a shout. "Hey!" It was Simon, calling from the loft window. He pointed to the sky. "Look up," he shouted. "The clouds are on fire."

Sure enough; the puffy clouds over town were glowing a deep orange. "Can you see what's causing it?" called Dill.

Simon leaned out the loft window. "There's smoke," he called. "Let's climb Cemetery Hill and see what's burning."

Dill pointed across the meadow. "Meet me on the far side of Horse Creek." She picked up the bucket of spring water and ran down the path.

At the house, Ma's eyes fluttered open. "Can you get me a drink?" she whispered.

Dill freshened her mother's water glass. She dipped a rag in the spring water. Ma sighed when she laid the cold compress on her forehead.

"That feels good," Ma said. She set her glass on the nightstand. "It's too painful to drink with this raw throat."

"Doc Miller said to wrap your neck with wool," said Dill.

Ma pointed to the foot of her bed. "Look in the cedar chest," she whispered.

The lid of Ma's chest opened easily. A silk scarf lay on top of her hand-stitched quilts. Dill ran her fingers over the shiny, yellow cloth. In happier times, the scarf's golden fringes had swirled through the air to the tune of flute and fiddle. Ma and Pa had never missed the Jackson County barn dance. Pa used to lift Dill in his arms and swing her around the dusty floor.

Dill sighed. Those times were gone, perhaps forever. She reached under the silk scarf for the gray woolen one and wrapped it around her mother's neck. Ma closed her eyes and coughed.

CHAPTER FOURTEEN

The clouds overhead cast an orange hue on the meadow grass. In the twilight, Dill could just make out Simon perched on a rock on the far side of Horse Creek. The forest behind him was growing dark.

Whippoorwill, whippoorwill, whippoorwill, came a call from deep in the woods. Simon stood and waved. "I was starting to worry you'd changed your mind," he said.

Who, whooo. Who, whooo. Simon turned and peered into the forest.

"C'mon," said Dill. She led the way, trotting along the stream to where the path turned into the woods. "Climb over this log," she said, hopping over a fallen tree.

The path zig-zagged through tall oaks and old maples. It crossed a narrow stream, then turned sharply up. "We're almost to Bat Rock," Dill said.

The path narrowed as it skirted the edge of a giant rock. The flutter of wings burst from a crack, surrounding them.

"What's that?" asked Simon.

"Stand still," said Dill. The bats flurried away as quickly as they had appeared. She grabbed Simon's hand, pulling him along the narrow path. They came to a spot where the trail switched back on itself, making a gradual climb up the hillside. "We can take these switchbacks," said Dill. "But we'll get there quicker if we go straight up."

"Let's get there as fast as we can," said Simon.

Dill grabbed the vines growing from the forest floor and pulled herself up the steep hillside. After a few minutes of climbing, the woods opened to a meadow. The last of the sun's rays lit up a row of tall cedars just below the hilltop. "We'll have to pass my uncle to get to the top," said Dill.

Simon raised his eyebrows. "Let's hurry," he said. "I don't want to be there when his ghost comes out."

Eight wooden crosses cast long shadows across the graves of the Union dead. Dill hurried to the stone of Jonah C. Jones and scrambled on top. Simon climbed up beside her. "Jackson's on fire!" he shouted.

Sure enough; a plume of gray smoke rose, like a chimney, from the far side of the courthouse.

A deep voice called out from the old sycamore. "What are you children doing up here?" Beside the tree's giant trunk Dill could just make out the silhouette of a man with a stovepipe hat.

Simon gasped. "It's your uncle's ghost."

"Is that the Dunbar girl?" called the voice.

Dill squinted. "Mr. Dickason?"

"Get home to your mother," called the man. "We've got enemy soldiers roaming the county."

"Who is it?" asked Simon.

"I think it's the county treasurer," said Dill.

"But why is he up here?" asked Simon. "All the other men are chopping trees on the road to town."

"Mr. Dickason?" called Dill. "Why are you here?"

Mr. Dickason took off his hat and leaned against the trunk of the old sycamore. "Haven't you heard?" he asked. "Morgan's Raiders marched all of Jackson's men to the fairgrounds; locked 'em up before they could drop a single log."

Dill's legs felt like limp noodles. She sat on the tombstone of Jonah C. Jones. "My brother was helping the sheriff," she said.

Mr. Dickason shook his head. "You'd better pray for his soul," he said. "General Morgan will decide in the morning whether to stand them before a firing squad or let them go."

Dill's chest tightened. She could not imagine life without Jim.

"Why are you hiding up here?" Simon asked.

Mr. Dickason patted a bag leaning against the sycamore trunk. "I took all the county's money from the bank vault," he said. "I'm hiding it here so the Rebels can't steal it." He stood and looked down the winding road. "Have you seen any sign they followed me?"

Simon shook his head. "They're too busy burning the town." He pointed in the distance. "Look!"

Mr. Dickason took a few steps up the hill. Orange flames leapt into the sky. "It's the train depot," he said. "The Rebels were fixing to set it on fire before I fled."

Sure enough; the flames were centered on the east side of town, near the granary. Mr. Dickson ran back to huddle beside his money. "You children go home," he shouted. "Don't tell a soul you saw me."

Simon grabbed Dill's sleeve, pulling her to her feet. "C'mon," he said. "There's nothing we can do about the fire."

Below Bat Rock, Simon turned up the path leading north. "I'm going to check on our farm. If everything's in place, I'll sneak to the fairgrounds and check on Pa and Jim."

"Do you think they're all right?"

Simon nodded. "They've got 'til morning," he said. "They'll outwit those stupid Rebels." He gave Dill a gentle push down the path. "Tend to your ma. I'll circle back when I've got something to report." He turned and disappeared into the darkening woods.

Dill felt her way through the woods. Just as the narrow path reached Horse Creek, Nellie's howl rose up through the trees. Dill stopped to listen. The beagle's shrill baying was too high-pitched to be about Jim riding up the lane.

Dill picked up her pace until she was racing along the creek. Across from their house, she crouched beside the flowing water and pushed aside a sumac branch. What she saw made her gasp. Two rows of men on horseback filled up their lane as far as she could see.

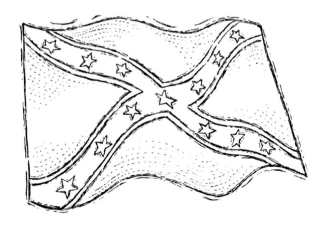

CHAPTER FIFTEEN

Dill's heart pounded against her ribs. An endless column of soldiers on horseback spilled into the yard. The riders weaved in and around one another such that determining their number was as difficult as counting tadpoles in a pail. Was General Morgan's entire army invading her farm?

Across the meadow, Ma's bedroom curtains hung open. Nellie's howls pierced the air. Could Ma be awake, watching from her bed?

Dill eyed her route to Grandpap's musket. Her heart sank. She could never make it to the barn without being seen by the enemy. If she could get to the house and pull Ma to her feet, they might slip across Salt Lick Creek and hide in the cornfield. But Doc Miller had warned against getting Ma out of bed.

As Dill watched, a cluster of soldiers separated from the others and rode across the meadow. Their horses stepped into the creek and stretched their slender necks to drink.

Dill scooted deeper into the woods to watch from the shadows. These men didn't look a thing like soldiers. Their pants were torn and ragged. Only two wore coats resembling uniforms. One had tall boots on his feet, but most wore ordinary shoes. Still others wore no shoes at all.

The riders' weapons were as different from each other as their clothing. Only two carried guns across their saddles. Two others had pistols tucked into belts. A long sword dangled from the belt of a man who leaned so far forward, Dill wondered if he might fall on his weapon and cut himself in two.

The horses finished drinking and wandered up the stream bank to nibble grass in the meadow. A soldier with a long musket poked the one with the sword. "Wake up," he said.

The other soldier sat up. "Huh? Where are we?"

"East side of Jackson. Ol' Morgan gave us eight hours to rest. Might as well lay your blanket out and sleep like a civilized man."

The sleepy soldier swung down from his horse. His legs crumpled, sending him to the ground with a thud. The other men laughed. "See here," said the man on the ground. "What do you expect after thirty-six hours in the saddle?"

A skinny soldier climbed off his horse and stumbled to the creek to kneel beside the water. "D'ya reckon the lady of this house kin cook?" he asked.

"Sure hope so," said the soldier on the ground. "I'd sell my own sister for a plate of biscuits 'n gravy."

"I'll eat anything but hardtack," said the skinny solider. He tossed a cracker in the creek. "Nearly broke a tooth on that worm castle." He scooped water with his hands, splashing his face. His shirt looked like Pa's old work shirt. His elbows poked through tattered holes in the sleeves.

Across the meadow, Nellie bayed at the heels of a Rebel marching toward the house with a flaming torch.

"No," Dill whispered. She crawled through the woods. When she reached the path along the creek, she stood and ran.

Nellie's howls grew higher pitched, until she was practically squealing. Through the woods Dill could see the man with the torch climbing the steps to the front porch. She ran to where the trail crossed their lane and ducked into Ma's vegetable garden, hiding behind the sweet corn. It was a quick dash to the woodpile, then up the back steps.

Once inside, Dill could hear the soldier's fist banging against the front door. A flame flickered in the parlor window. Dill burst into her mother's bedroom. "Get up," she called. "The Rebels are setting fire to the house!"

CHAPTER SIXTEEN

"Light a candle," Ma whispered.

Dill carried a candle to the kitchen hearth and touched it to the coals. The candle burst into flames. She stuck it in the candleholder and hurried back to her mother's side.

Ma sat up and unwrapped the wool scarf. Dill gasped. Her mother's neck looked like a summer squash that had been left in the garden too long, it was so big around.

"What's wrong?" asked Ma.

"Look," said Dill, holding up a hand mirror.

Ma ran her hand over her swollen neck. "If that ain't a sight," she rasped.

A fist pounded the front door. "Open up," called a voice. "Who's at the door?" asked Ma.

"It's the Rebels," said Dill. "Go to the door while I run to the barn for the gun."

Dill stepped into the hall. The silhouette of a man appeared in the window, then disappeared. He pounded the door so hard, Dill feared he might break it down. "Open this door," he shouted.

Ma leaned back on her pillow. "I'm too weak to get out of bed," she said. "Tell him your mother has diphtheria. That will scare him away."

Dill lifted the candleholder from the nightstand. She stopped beside Ma's mirror to straighten her collar before heading down the hall.

From the other side of the front door, Nellie let out a squeal. Dill unlocked the door and peered out. Nellie darted through the crack. The scruff of her neck stood straight up.

A soldier in a gray coat pushed the door open with his boot and stepped inside. "Hello young lady," he said, removing his hat. "I am Lieutenant Joshua Crumm of the Confederate States of America."

Dill raised her eyebrows. "Good evening, sir," she said. Her voice sounded stronger than she felt inside.

The soldier placed his hat back on his head. "What's your name, little miss?"

"Cordelia," said Dill. "Cordelia Dunbar."

"A pleasure to meet you, Miss Cordelia. Now, if you would be so kind as to fetch your mother, I wish to ask a favor."

"My ma's sick," said Dill. "It's diphtheria."

Lt. Crumm stepped backward until he was standing on the porch. "Is there anyone else at home? An aunt, perhaps, or an older sister?"

Dill shook her head. "My Pa's off fighting in the war and my brother . . ." She stopped. If Rebels were at her door, it meant Mr. Dickason was right. Jim was a prisoner of war.

The soldier's blue eyes twinkled in the torchlight. "I was hoping your mama might cook us some breakfast."

"In the middle of the night?"

The lieutenant nodded. "My men've ridden three days without a break. They need rest. We'll leave tomorrow, after a big Yankee breakfast."

"But it's treason to help the enemy," said Dill

Lt. Crumm's smile sent a shiver down Dill's back. "Let me explain this to you, Miss Cordelia. Either you fix us breakfast or I let this pack of hungry men find their own food." He looked down the hall toward the kitchen.

Dill walked past the lieutenant to the edge of the porch. She could see the silhouettes of horses. "How many are in your company?"

"Fifty-two," said the Rebel.

"You want me to cook a meal for fifty-two soldiers?"

Lieutenant Crumm nodded. "Where I come from, young ladies are right handy in the kitchen."

Dill thought of the bag of cornmeal her mother kept in the kitchen, 'Enough to feed a small army,' Pa used to say. She would have to cook it all. The three baskets of eggs in the cellar would merely whet the appetites of this many soldiers.

Dill held up her candle until she was looking directly into the lieutenant's eyes. "If I fix you breakfast, will you keep your men from stealing from us and promise not to burn our farm to the ground?"

The lieutenant smiled. His gold tooth glittered in the torchlight. "That depends," he said. "What will you fix?"

"I can bake cornbread and boil enough eggs for every man to have one, maybe two."

Lt. Crumm scratched a spot on his forehead. "Where I'm from, a farm like yours would have a smokehouse with a ham hung up to cure."

"I can offer a ham," said Dill. "If you promise to leave the rest of our farm alone."

"You've got yourself a bargain," said Lt. Crumm. "One more thing," he added. "Can I trouble you for a few dozen candles?"

Dill looked at the candle in her hand. She had helped her mother pour the wax for two dozen just last week. "I'll get you some candles."

Lt. Crumm took Dill's hand. "Thank you," he said. "We'll eat at dawn."

Dill shut the door and hurried back to Ma's room. Her mother sat up in bed. "Sounds like they're here 'til morning," she whispered.

"They want breakfast," said Dill.

Ma leaned back on her pillow. "That gives me a few hours to rest," she said. "Run and get the candles. If we're lucky, they'll be too tired to pick apart our farm."

In her mother's pantry, Dill counted out twelve candles. When she returned to the front porch, the lieutenant was gone. His men had fanned out across the farmyard. They slept beside their horses, some on bedrolls, others in the grass. Their horses slept, too, standing up.

As Dill and Nellie walked past the camped men, a soldier rolled over and reached for his bayonet. Dill wrapped an arm around Nellie. "Are the candles for us?" asked the soldier, reaching out his hand.

He flipped over his bayonet, jabbing the sharp end in the ground. The candle fit into the rounded end like it was made to hold candles. The other candles disappeared into the dark, then reappeared, stuck into bayonets. Their soft glow made the farmyard look more like a church gathering than a Rebel camp.

"S'cuse me," said a voice. "Do you have any more of them candles?"

Dill held her candle up to a man's bearded face. His eyes were weary from days in the saddle. He pointed to a spot beyond the well. "My nephew is ailing over yonder," he said. "I could use some candlelight to tend to him."

Dill followed the man to a gray blanket wrapped so tightly around a soldier you'd've thought it was a snowy winter night. She held the candle over the blanket. The soldier's head stuck out one end, his dusty boots out the other. His blond hair was plastered to his forehead. His cheeks glowed red as cherries. The soldier in the blanket coughed and gasped for breath. "It's diphtheria," whispered Dill.

The older man's eyes grew wide in the candlelight. "How d'ya know?"

"My ma's got the same red cheeks. Is his neck swollen?"

The boy's uncle unwrapped his blanket. "Will you look at that," he said. His nephew's neck was bigger around than Ma's.

"Shall I send for Doc Miller?" asked Dill.

The soldier shook his head. "Your Yankee doctor'd sooner jail the boy as cure him."

The young soldier turned his head and spat in the grass. He coughed so hard, Dill thought he might split in two.

"He's my sister's boy," said the bearded soldier. "He just turned sixteen last week. Not a hint of peach fuzz on his chin. I should never have let him join Morgan's army."

Dill thought of her own uncle. If Jim had marched off to war and come down with diphtheria, Uncle Swinge would've been desperate to help him. "Cold water from our spring will bring down his fever," she said.

The bearded soldier picked up a tin pot from beside his bedroll. "Where is your spring?"

"I need fresh water, for my ma," said Dill. "I'll take you there."

"Lead the way," he said.

Dill carried the candle to the well to collect Nellie's water pan. She trotted the Rebel up the path to the barn and down the other side between rows of corn. The soldier's boots pounded the trail behind her.

"This way," said Dill, turning toward the willow thicket. There, across the path, lay the switch Simon had used to cover their footprints. Dill gasped. In her rush to help the young Rebel, she was leading his uncle straight to Buck.

CHAPTER SEVENTEEN

The dirt turned cool under Dill's bare feet. Her mind raced for a way to keep the soldier from finding Buck. She slowed to a walk.

"Lawd have mercy, Miss," said the bearded Rebel. "Why're you slowing down?"

"I left a batch of biscuits over the fire," said Dill. She turned to face the Rebel. "I have to go back, before they burn."

An owl hooted from deep in the darkness. The Rebel strained to see into the willow thicket. "I hear water gurgling." He reached for the candle in Dill's hand. "Give me that," he said. "I'll get the water myself."

Dill stepped back. "It's my candle," she said. "And my family's spring. Give me your pot. I'll get the water."

The Rebel grabbed Dill's arm and lowered the candle toward the ground. "Well, I'll be darned," he said. "I thought I smelled mint."

Sure enough; they were standing smack dab in the middle of Pa's peppermint patch. "My pa planted this patch of mint back when he built the spring house."

The soldier yanked a handful of mint from the ground. "Tell me about the stream running out of your spring?" he asked. "Does it have a muddy bank?"

Dill flicked a chunk of dry mud from her leg. She and Simon had stepped through ankle-deep mud to get Buck to the far side of the cave. "It's muddy all right," she said. "Why are you asking?"

The Rebel held the mint to Dill's face. "With this mint and some cool mud, we can make the best cure I know for a fever."

Dill stared into the Rebel's face. "I never heard of using mud to cure a fever."

"Take me to your spring," he said. "I'll show you."

Dill looked down the trail. It might be possible to collect mud and spring water without giving away Buck's hiding spot. After all, he was hidden on the far side of the pool. If this Rebel's cure could bring down Ma's fever, it would be worth the risk.

"All right," said Dill. "Let's be quick about it."

The mud softened under their feet as the gurgling grew louder. Dill stopped beside the spring pool and held her candle close to the water.

The Rebel grabbed a stick. "Hold the candle, while I stir up the bottom."

Dill let out her breath. The Rebel would never see across the pool if she held the candle near the water. Buck was safe.

The soldier stirred the bottom, making thick muddy waves. Once the water was brown, he picked up his tin pot. "You've got bare feet," he said. "Step in and dip the pot in the water."

Dill stepped into the cold water. A soft snort floated across the pool. The soldier peered into the darkness. "What was that?"

Dill's stomach sunk to her knees. "There's a family of raccoons down here," she said. "It must've been one them."

The Rebel shrugged. He shoved the stick back into the mud and stirred. The pool grew cloudier. "Now," he said. "Dip in the pot."

Dill dropped the tin pot in the water "Got it," she said.

The Rebel looked into the pot. "That's not enough mud."

"Sure it is," said Dill.

"It'll take more than that for two people," he said. "Dip it again, deeper this time."

Dill glanced across the pool. "This is enough," she said. "Let's go."

The Rebel took the pot and dumped out the water. "Dip it again," he said. "In the muddiest spot."

Dill stared into the darkness. She willed Buck not to move. "All right," she said.

The Rebel stirred up the water again. Dill dipped the pot in the darkest, brownest spot. The soldier took the tin pot and handed her Nellie's drinking pan. "This one, too," he said.

Dill filled the second pot with water. "There," said the Rebel. "That should be enough."

Dill stepped out of the pool. "Let's go," she said.

A whinny rose up from across the pool. The sound echoed off the rock wall, repeating until it faded into the willow thicket. The Rebel pulled the candle from Dill's hand. "If I was a betting man, I'd bet $100 you're hiding a horse down here."

He held the candle over his head and walked around the edge of the pool. The shadow of a horse appeared on the back wall of the cave. The Rebel laughed. "Will you look at that," he said. "I'll bet you another $100 there ain't no biscuits cookin' in your kitchen."

Dill grabbed Buck's lead rope. "You can't have him," she said.

The soldier admired Buck in the candlelight. He ran a hand across his firm back and down his flank.

"Lt. Crumm promised you wouldn't steal from our farm," said Dill. "That includes horses."

The Rebel carried the candle behind Buck. "I'd never consider stealing another man's horse in peacetime." His voice echoed off the rocks. "But in my situation, a horse like this could mean the difference between getting home or rotting in a Yankee prison."

Dill watched the Rebel examine Jim's horse. He looked at the bottoms of Buck's feet. He pried open his lips to inspect his teeth.

Dill tugged on the Rebel's coat. "Let's get back to the house," she said. "Your nephew needs this cold mud."

"A few more minutes won't make a difference," said the Rebel.

"It sure will," said Dill. "He's sicker than my ma. Besides, Buck ain't going nowhere. He'll be fine in the hollow 'til morning,"

The soldier smiled. "I know what you're up to, little lady."

"It'll cause quite a commotion if you bring a horse like Buck into the yard," said Dill.

The Rebel patted Buck's jaw. "You've got a point," he said. "They're all asleep, except for Crumm. Can't let the lieutenant make off with my prize horse."

Dill picked up her pot of muddy water. "I s'pect your nephew's shaking all over with fever."

The Rebel held the candle up to Buck. He ran his hand down the horse's neck. "Shame to leave such a fine animal in this damp holler," he said. "But I s'pose there's no harm in letting him stay here 'til morning."

Dill didn't wait for the Rebel to reconsider. She ran up the path. At the top of the hill, she stopped beside the barn. Small circles of candlelight cast their glow on sleeping soldiers. A campfire flickered beside the buggy shed. From somewhere across the meadow, a slow fiddle tune floated through the night air.

In a few short hours, the sun would rise. The soldiers camped on her farm would demand breakfast. In return, they might leave her farm as they found it. Or they might burn it to the ground.

Dill wished the musket in the loft was a cannon. She wished she could run into the woods and never look back. Neither of those wishes was about to come true. She took a deep breath and hurried down the path to the house.

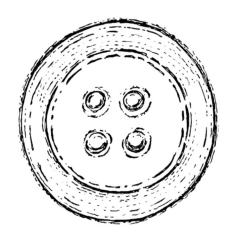

CHAPTER EIGHTEEN

The bearded Rebel pulled the bayonet off his rifle and jammed it into the ground next to his nephew. Dill stuck the candle in the end. The yellow flame lit up the boy's flushed face. His eyes were squeezed shut, his breathing slow and raspy.

"Have you got something to grind these mint leaves?" asked the boy's uncle.

Dill ran into the house. She went first to Ma's bedroom. Her mother slept fitfully, coughing between breaths. "I'll be back," she whispered.

In the kitchen, Dill found the mortar and pestle Ma used for grinding spices. She carried them outside to where the young soldier lay wrapped in his blanket. The bearded Rebel filled the mortar with mint leaves. "Grind these up," he said. "Until they're nothing but green pulp."

He pulled a handful of mud from the bottom of the tin pail and mixed it with enough cold water to make a thin paste. Dill scraped the green pulp into the paste to make a minty poultice.

The older soldier pointed to a dented canteen tied to the boy's leather pack. "I'm going to fill the boy's canteen with well water," he said. "Start spreading the poultice on his face and neck. The mint should open his throat so he can drink. The poor lad hasn't swallowed a drop all day."

Dill stared at the bearded man's nephew. His fair complexion made him look much younger than Jim. The wool blanket was wrapped so tightly around his neck, Dill had to tug it apart. The butternut coat underneath was frayed at the neck. Small patches covered holes in the chest and shoulder. Rusty pinholes stood up on the coat's left breast where medals had once hung. Had this old coat been worn by another soldier in a war long ago?

Dill unbuttoned the coat's tarnished buttons. Underneath, the young soldier wore a shirt of coarse muslin held together by neat rows of stitches. The shirt's delicate buttons, cut from the shells of oysters, gave off a lustrous glow in the candlelight. Dill unbuttoned the top button. She dipped her hand in the mint poultice and spread it on the young man's flushed face. There was so little hair on his chin, it was like caring for a child. A smile flickered across his lips. "Mama," he whispered.

"I ain't your Ma," said Dill. "But I'll do what I can to fix you up." She loosened a second button in his muslin shirt and spread cold mud on his neck.

When she'd thoroughly coated his neck and chin, Dill closed up the young Rebel's shirt. The top button fell off in her fingers. She turned it over, admiring its mother-of-pearl glow. The lady who had stitched together the young man's shirt would want to sew this button back on when he returned from war.

Dill unbuttoned a third tarnished button on the butternut coat. Her pa's Union officer coat had secret pockets sewn into the lining. This soldier's coat must have secret pockets, too. Sure enough; Dill spotted a small opening in the coat's tan lining. She slipped her fingers between the satin layers and dropped the button inside.

Something in the secret pocket poked her fingertip. She spread the layers of lining and peeked inside. The corner of a paper stuck up from the little pocket.

Dill wiped her fingers in the grass. She pulled the folded paper from the pocket and opened it under the candle. Three lines of blue ink flowed in a woman's delicate handwriting.

Caleb William Christianson.
Son of Amos and Omey Christianson.
If killed in battle, send body home to Stanton, Kentucky.

The blood rushed to Dill's face. She read the words again. *If killed in battle, send body home.* Tears stung her eyes. This soldier was too young to die. She slid the paper back inside the pocket and buttoned up the butternut coat.

A muddy boot stepped through the grass, stopping next to Dill. "Now don't he look pretty?" Dill looked up into the eyes of Caleb Christianson's uncle. "Good heavens, Miss," he gasped. "What's wrong?"

Dill swallowed hard. "I found his paper tag."

"What the devil are you talking about?"

"His tag," said Dill.

The older soldier frowned.

"There's a note inside his coat telling where to send his body," said Dill. A lump filled her throat. "If he's killed in battle."

She unbuttoned Caleb's tattered coat and pointed to the secret pocket. The bearded Rebel unfolded the paper and held it beside the candle. "Ain't that just like my little sister?" he said. "Makin' sure her boy comes home one way or t'other." He pulled a wrinkled handkerchief from his pocket and wiped his eyes. "The boy's gonna be fine," he said. "Now that you're fixing him up."

Dill wiped her face with the back of her hand. "My ma got my Uncle Swinge's paper tag." She pointed to the hill across Horse Creek. "He's buried up there, on Cemetery Hill."

The Rebel shook his head. "I hate this war. It's serving nobody and hurtin' folks on both sides." He handed Dill his handkerchief. "What's your name, little lady?"

Dill took the Rebel's handkerchief. "Cordelia," she whispered. She dipped the wrinkled cloth in spring water and spread it over Caleb's forehead.

"I'm Levi Long," said the Rebel. "And this here is Caleb. I'm sorry you lost your uncle."

"He was shot through the belly by a Minié ball."

Levi Long spat on the ground. "Curse those Miniés. I wish to God they'd never been invented."

Dill glared at Levi Long. "But you Rebels invented them."

The Rebel's mouth hung open. "Is that what they're telling you Yankee children? That Minié balls were dreamed up by southern folks?"

Dill nodded. "It's true, ain't it?"

Levi Long shook his head. "A Frenchman invented them," he said. "And your Union soldiers have been shootin' 'em at our boys ever since you started this war." He pointed to Caleb. "Besides, d'ya think we're so evil as to make a piece of lead to tear apart a boy like him?"

Dill picked at one of the patches in Caleb's worn coat. "I s'pect you'd do anything to hang onto your colored folks."

Levi Long chuckled. "You mean our slaves?"

Dill nodded. "That's why my pa is fighting. So you'll free your slaves."

Levi Long slapped his knee. "Miss Cordelia, I wish you could see my farm. My house ain't no bigger than yours. 'Bout the only thing's different between my farm and yours is we have a barn 'specially for birthin' horses. But one thing you won't find on my property is slave quarters."

"You don't own any slaves?"

Caleb's uncle shook his head. "Never have. Never will."

"Then why're you fighting in this war?"

Levi Long sat down in the grass. "There's more to this war than freeing slaves, Miss Cordelia. Much more, like states' rights. But the main reason Caleb and I are camped in your yard tonight is because we're admirers of General John Hunt Morgan. When the general called for an army, I jumped on my horse. Caleb, too." He looked down at his nephew. "Well I'll be darned. That peppermint poultice is doin' its trick. Look."

For the first time since Dill had laid eyes on him, Caleb's face was not twisted in pain. His chest rose and fell without a struggle. Dill picked up Nellie's dented water pan. "Your poultice worked," she said. "I'm going to coat my ma with it."

Dill took one step inside the back door and froze. Ma stood in the hall with a candle. "Where's your brother?" she asked.

CHAPTER NINETEEN

Ma looked like she'd been cooking over a hot fire, her face was so flushed with fever. The flame of the candle flickered from her shaking hand. "Jim hasn't come back from town," said Dill.

Ma collapsed into a chair and leaned her head in her hands. "What's to become of us?"

Dill rested her hand on her mother's shoulder. "Remember, Ma? I talked to the lieutenant. All they want is a place to rest." She paused. "And breakfast, when the sun comes up."

Ma nodded. "I don't know how we're going to feed this many men."

"It's been most of a week since Jim has traded in town," said Dill. "We've got three full baskets of eggs in the cellar. We can boil the eggs, mix up some cornbread, and cut up a ham from the smokehouse."

Ma's body shook with chills. "Look at me," she said. "I won't be much help."

Dill hugged her mother. "If we can bring down your fever maybe you'll feel better in time to cook breakfast."

Ma put an arm around Dill's shoulders. "Help me into bed."

Dill helped her mother down the hall. She eased her into bed and pulled the blankets around her chin. She hurried back to the kitchen and ground up the rest of the mint leaves. When she returned with the pan, she said, "This cold mud poultice worked for a sick Rebel. Shall I smear some on you?"

Ma scowled. "You want to coat me with mud?"

"There's a boy sicker than you lying out there," said Dill. "This poultice helped him breathe."

Ma leaned back on her pillow. "All right," she said. "But don't get the linens dirty."

Dill spread mud across her mother's cheeks and forehead. The muscles in Ma's face relaxed. She shut her eyes. "It feels good," she said. By the time Dill had coated her chin and neck, she was fast asleep.

Dill washed her hands in the basin. She opened the cupboard and pulled out the bag of cornmeal. All the while, her mind raced with thoughts of Buck. If she left him in the hollow, Levi Long would steal him. She had to find a new hiding place. But where? He was too big to fit in the hen house. She stirred flour and lard into the cornmeal. Next came the eggs. She might as well bring up all three baskets from the cellar. Aha! That was it! The Rebels would never look for a horse in an earthen cellar.

Dill opened the back door and leapt off the step. She tiptoed past the well so as not to wake the soldiers sleeping around it. They were camped in front of the buggy shed, too. Dill ran behind it and opened the doors to the cellar.

The corridor wall felt cool as she slid her hand along it. The dark space was perfect for hiding a horse. When she got to where the corridor opened into the cellar, she reached a hand above her head. She could not touch the ceiling, even when she stood on her toes. She would have to trick Buck to get him down the steps. But he would fit in the cellar.

She ran the egg baskets to the house and set them in the kitchen. Her ma slept, breathing easier than she had all night. She would never miss the candle on her nightstand. Dill carried the candle up the path to the barn and down past the cornfield. Once in the willow thicket, she let out a low whistle. A soft snort answered from across the pool.

"I'm back," said Dill, running up to Buck. She set down the candle and untied the rope. "Let's get you out of this muddy hollow." Buck pushed his muzzle into Dill's chest and snorted.

The sky above Cemetery Hill was still dark as Dill led Buck up the path to the barn. She wrapped the rope around the corner post of his pen and scooted between the rails. By candlelight, she lifted the oat bag from its nail.

She trotted Buck to the back side of the hill and opened the cellar doors. The doorway looked smaller now that Buck was with her. She held up the oat bag. When he leaned down to nibble, she pulled on the rope. Buck stepped down one step, then two. Dill kissed his muzzle.

At the third step, she offered a handful of oats. She led him down the narrow tunnel to the chamber filled with Ma's pickles and preserves. Dill stroked Buck's flank. It was a tight fit, but he was hidden where no Rebel could see or hear him. She opened the oat bag and set it on the dirt floor. "Eat all you want," she said. "I'll be back in a few hours."

Dill lifted the last basket of eggs and ran outside, closing the doors behind her. The first hint of light was erasing the stars from the night sky as she passed the well. She smiled. All she had to do now was fix breakfast for fifty-two enemy soldiers.

CHAPTER TWENTY

"Dill," Ma whispered. "Can you get me a drink?"

Four muffled chimes sounded from the bureau. Dill handed her mother the glass. Ma touched the water to her lips and shook her head. "I can only swallow a sip," she said. "I don't see how I can make breakfast."

Dill stared at her mother.

"Do you remember how to make cornbread?" Ma asked.

"Yes, ma'am," said Dill.

"Each of my Dutch ovens will hold enough to feed twenty men."

Dill thought of her multiplication tables. It would take two and a half batches of cornbread to feed fifty-two men. If she cooked three batches, there would be some left over for when Jim returned from Jackson. If Jim returned. The blood throbbed in Dill's temples. She could not think of her brother right now.

"Build up the fire," said Ma. "So you can boil the eggs first."

"Yes'm," said Dill. "A big fire means lots of coals for baking."

Ma smiled. "You're a smart girl, Cordelia," she said, shutting her eyes. Within seconds she was asleep.

What with all the commotion, the fire had not been lit for nearly 24 hours. Jim had banked the ashes the way Pa had taught him. One ember still glowed cherry red. Dill laid a piece of dry kindling on the ember and blew on it. The kindling burst into flames.

Quickly, Dill built up a tower of wood from the box beside the hearth. In no time, she had a roaring fire. She hung her mother's largest kettle from the hook and poured in water from the bucket beside the washbasin. Two trips to the well and the kettle was full. Once the water began to boil, she would drop in the first basket of eggs to boil.

Next, Dill measured out more cornmeal and chose half a dozen eggs from the basket. Ma always broke the eggs. Dill held her breath and tapped the first egg on the edge of the bowl. The eggshell broke clean letting the yolk drop into the cornmeal. When she tapped the second egg, a chunk of shell dropped into the bowl. She reached to pick it out, then stopped. These Rebels were not her guests. She smiled as she stirred the shell into the cornmeal. She took less care cracking the rest of the eggs. Three more chunks of shell fell into the bowl. Dill folded the eggshell into the mixture. She added the lard, salt, and saleratus, so the cornbread would rise. Finally she added the sour milk and finished stirring.

Dill greased her mother's two Dutch ovens and poured in the yellow batter. On any other day, two pans of cornbread sitting in the fireplace meant company was coming for breakfast. Not today.

The eggs would soon be boiling. Once they were finished, she could knock down the fire and stack coals on the Dutch ovens. She would need more eggs to make the third batch of cornbread. It had been over twelve hours since she'd been to the hen house. Surely the chickens had laid more eggs.

The sky was turning light as Dill stepped out the back door. Nellie jumped up from her spot beside the rain barrel. The basket in Dill's hand told the beagle she was headed to the hen house. Sleeping men lay on either side of them as Nellie led the way up the path. The little beagle lifted her nose, sniffing each one as she passed. Could she smell the fires they had set to innocent farms or the prize horses they had stolen?

At the hen house door, Dill stopped. She wanted Nellie by her side, but dogs don't belong in chicken houses. She knelt by the door. "I'll be right back," she said.

The hens slept in their nests as if nothing was amiss. They didn't pay Dill any mind as she reached under them.

When she'd finished collecting enough eggs for cornbread, she heard Nellie yelp.

A man's voice snarled, "Get outta the way, you mongrel."

Dill ducked behind a wooden crate. The door to the hen house swung open. A man stepped inside. "I'll wring they necks," he said. "You pluck they feathers."

"Don't care whether I'm wringin' or pluckin'," said a deeper voice. "Just want to eat me some white meat."

A chicken flapped and flew to a roost overhead. "Grab it!" said the first man.

The chicken next to Dill flapped from of its nest and hovered a few feet off the ground. A dark figure grabbed the hen, making it squawk.

Dill jumped to her feet. "Let her go!"

The man holding the hen jumped.

"What is it?" asked the deep voice.

The man with the hen bent over Dill. He squinted in the dark. "Believe it's a girl."

Dill stepped onto the crate, making her stand as tall as the man. "You can't eat our laying hens," she said.

The soldier laughed. "Layin' hens are tough. We're looking for a nice, young pullet."

Dill waved her finger. "Lt. Crumm promised you wouldn't raid our farm."

"What'd she say, Jeb?"

The man with the hen laughed. "She says Crumm promised we'd leave her hens alone."

The man by the door snorted. "Crumm don't know all what goes on in this company."

Dill hopped off the wooden crate. She pushed past the chicken thieves. "C'mon, Nellie," she said.

The sky over Cemetery Hill was turning pink. It would soon be dawn. The lieutenant would expect his breakfast.

Dill ran to where a cluster of Rebels gathered around the rain barrel. Their long coats hung from the branches of the walnut tree. One man sharpened a razor on a strap while another tacked a mirror to the tree. Dill thought of her pa. What would he think if he knew a party of Rebels was setting up at his favorite shaving spot?

Lt. Crumm sniffed at the open window. "I smell our breakfast cooking," he said.

Dill shoved through the men until she was standing before the lieutenant. "Tell your men to stop raiding our farm," she said, "or I ain't feeding you breakfast."

"Why, Miss Cordelia," said Lt. Crumm. "Is something the matter?" He swished his shaving brush in his cup, filling it with white bubbles.

"You'd better call off your men," said Dill.

A soldier beside the rain barrel laughed. "That's right, Crumm," he said. "Call off yer men."

Lt. Crumm's eyebrows bunched into a knot. "Are my men misbehaving, Miss Cordelia?"

"They certainly are," said Dill. "I found two of 'em in our hen house, fixing to pluck and fry up one of our laying hens."

"If that's all they're doing, you should consider yourself lucky," said a soldier.

"Quiet," said Lt. Crumm. He turned to Dill. "What did you say you'd fix for breakfast?"

"Cornbread and eggs."

"And smoked ham?"

"I'm fixing to keep my side of the bargain. But your men have to stop raiding our farm."

Lt. Crumm climbed the steps to the back door and let out a whistle so loud, you could've heard it in Pike County. Soldiers across the yard crawled from their sleeping rolls and wandered over to the rain barrel.

In the pale light, Crumm's men appeared more ragged than they'd looked in the dark. Some wore gray jackets with medals. Others' jackets were butternut brown, like Caleb's. Only a few men's pants matched their coats. They scratched their heads so much, you'd've thought they had fleas. Dill recognized Levi Long in the second row. She wondered if he had gone back to the cave spring to look for Buck.

Lt. Crumm gestured at Dill. "Our hostess, Miss Cordelia, has agreed to cook a Yankee breakfast of ham 'n eggs and cornbread," he said. "With such a generous offer, there's no need to raid her family's stores."

"We was fixin' to fry up this young hen," said a voice. The shorter of the men from the hen house held a chicken by the feet.

"Put the hen back," said Lt. Crumm. He turned to Dill. "What about the ham?"

"I'll need help cutting it down from the hook in our smokehouse," said Dill.

Lt. Crumm pointed to a barefooted man in the front row. "Go help the girl," he said.

A familiar voice spoke up from the back row. "I'll help her," said Levi Long. He pushed his way up to the rain barrel. "Cordelia brought down Caleb's fever in the night. The least I can do is help her get a ham."

The throng of hungry soldiers wandered back to their campsites.

"Thank you," said Dill. She led Levi Long past the hen house. He did not mention Buck. "How's Caleb?" she asked when they'd rounded the buggy shed.

"Still not out of the woods, but better. And your ma?"

"She's better, too. Your mint poultice helped her sleep."

Dill opened the smokehouse door. "I s'pect we ought to cut down the biggest one," she said, pointing to a ham that was bigger than Nellie.

Levi pulled his knife from its sheaf. "Get under it," he said. The knife blade sliced through the rope, dropping the ham into Dill's arms. "You want me to carry it?" he asked.

"No," said Dill. "My pa cured this ham. I want to keep it in my arms as long as I can."

Levi Long pushed the smokehouse door open with his foot. "I'm glad we got a chance to talk," he said. "I've been thinking about your horse."

Dill felt a pang of guilt. She waited for Levi Long to say Buck was missing.

He lifted his hat and scratched his head. "I'm going to leave him in the hollow."

Dill looked into the bearded Rebel's eyes. "Why did you change your mind?" she asked. "Are you ashamed to steal him?"

Levi Long shook his head. "I've stolen plenty of horses on this raid." He laid a hand on Dill's shoulder. "Caleb talked me out of it."

"What?" asked Dill.

Levi Long looked toward the spot where his nephew slept. "Caleb had a sister named Melissa who died of the scarlet fever a few winters back," he said. "Last night, she came to him in a fever dream. She told him he would survive the diphtheria."

The first rays of sunlight crested Cemetery Hill, turning Dill's house a soft pink. "I never heard of such a thing," said Dill. "I wonder if my ma was visited by my uncle."

"There's more," said Levi Long. "Melissa told Caleb to pay a kindness to the one who brought down his fever." He squeezed Dill's shoulder. "That's you, Miss Cordelia."

Dill's heart leapt to think she could keep Buck. "C'mon," she said, lifting the ham. "Let's get your army fed so you can be on your way."

The lieutenant was finishing his shave when Dill got back to the house. "Here," she said, handing over the ham. "Have your men slice this up while I spoon eggs from the water."

"How soon will we get a taste of that cornbread?" he asked.

Dill smiled. "As soon as it's done baking."

Lt. Crumm tipped his hat. "Much obliged, Miss Cordelia."

Back in the kitchen, bubbles boiled up through the eggs in Ma's big pot. Dill scooped more cornmeal and flour into a bowl and broke three more eggs. A piece of eggshell fell into the bowl. She dipped it out with a spoon, before stirring in the lard and sour milk.

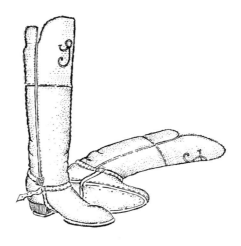

CHAPTER TWENTY-ONE

The sky over Cemetery Hill was turning blue as Dill stepped out the back door with a platter of cornbread and a basket of steaming eggs. She passed through the yard, stepping over bedrolls and muskets. "Much obliged," said a man in a butternut coat and gray pants.

"Thanky, little lady," said a Rebel who had taken his gun apart to clean it.

The soldiers who had been in the chicken house helped themselves to cornbread. Dill hoped they each got big chunks of eggshell.

On the far side of the well, Levi Long dozed on his gray blanket. Caleb lay on his bedroll, his head propped up on a knapsack. The boy's eyes were as blue as the morning sky, his face pale. The swelling in his neck had gone down a bit. "How're you feeling?" asked Dill.

Caleb touched the cracked mud on his neck. "You the girl that coated me with this?" he whispered.

Dill nodded.

"Thank you," he said.

"Do you think you can eat a little egg and cornbread?"

Caleb shook his blond head.

Levi Long opened his eyes. "I got him to swallow some water a while back," he said. "Sure wish he'd at least try to eat somethin'."

Dill offered the plate of cornbread to Levi Long. He broke off a piece and held it to his nephew's mouth. Caleb coughed hard, sending yellow crumbs across his bedroll. "Can't get a thing down this throat," he whispered. "Hurts just to drink." He laid his head back and shut his eyes.

Levi took two eggs from the basket. "Guess I'll eat mine and his."

Dill looked down at Caleb. "I don't see how he's going to ride away from here."

"He can't ride," said Levi Long. "Not in his condition."

Dill thought about Levi's decision to leave Buck. "I'd offer you our wagon." She paused. "But I don't know how my brother could harvest the crops."

Levi ran his fingers through his beard. "Don't you worry, Miss Cordelia," he said. "I'll think of something."

Inside the house, Ma's face looked pasty white. Dill held a glass to her lips. She forced each sip down with a frown. "Can't take another swallow," she said, pushing the glass away.

A merry tune drifted in the open window. Dill peeked around the curtains. A handful of Rebels gathered around a man playing a fiddle. A tall soldier danced a jig. Another man tapped the backs of two spoons together, hitting them against his leg in a catchy rhythm. Lt. Crumm stood to one side, tapping his foot. Ma lifted herself on an elbow. "Who's that making music?"

Dill pulled her mother's curtains back so she could see from her bed. Clusters of soldiers were scattered from near the house to the far side of the meadow. The smell of sizzling ham floated in the window from their small campfires. Half a dozen ragged men stood beside the well washing their faces and rinsing out shirts.

"Good Lord," whispered Ma. She looked through the bedroom door to the parlor. "Is Jim home yet?"

Dill dropped the curtain. She couldn't tell Ma what Mr. Dickason had said about Gen. Morgan holding the town's men, not while she was so sick.

"Jim joined Sheriff Selfridge last night, west of town. They were going to chop down trees across the road to stop the Rebels from coming." She motioned out the window. "I guess the sheriff's plan didn't work."

Ma's eyes flashed with anger. "Jim's just a boy. The sheriff had no business calling on him." Her breath caught on the last words making her cough. She leaned back on her pillow. "What have they stolen?"

Dill smiled. "Once they knew I was fixin' up their breakfast, they settled down and left things alone."

"Have they found our silver?"

Dill nearly laughed. "They haven't even looked for it."

Ma fingered the dried mud on her face. "What have I got all over me?"

"Don't you remember?" asked Dill. "One of the Rebels taught me how to make a poultice out of mud and mint. I coated your face and throat with it in the night. It helped you sleep."

"Well," said Ma. "I'd like to wash it off. Get me a rag."

Dill went into the pantry to get a fresh rag. The water in the basin had grown warm overnight. She grabbed the kitchen pail and headed out the back door.

The Rebels at the well tipped their hats. "Mighty fine breakfast, young lady," said a soldier with gray hair.

A whoop rose up from the meadow. A group of men playing tug-of-war pulled a second group down the banks of Horse Creek and into the water. They slapped each other's backs, laughing. Across the creek, the flicker of something white caught Dill's eye. A shock of blond hair darted between two trees. A face appeared, then disappeared into the woods.

Dill grinned. Simon was back. She carried the bucket of water into the house to fill the basin. "Simon is hiding in the woods," she said, handing her mother a wet rag. "I've got to get to him before he does something foolish."

"Go on," whispered Ma. "I can wash my own face."

Dill took one step out the front door and stopped. Lt. Crumm sat on the bench. "I suppose you're wondering why I'm not getting my men ready to ride," he said.

Dill gave an awkward nod. She glanced across the meadow. There was no sign of Simon.

"I'm awaiting word from the general," said Crumm. He peeled a boiled egg. "Nice little farm you've got here, Miss Cordelia. Reminds me of my home in Kentucky."

Dill laid a hand on the porch rail. "Kentucky's just across the river. Why don't you cross back over?"

"All part of General Morgan's plan," said Crumm. He bit into the egg. "If things go as planned, we'll be home in time for Sunday supper."

A familiar ache came over Dill. "I wish my Pa could come home for Sunday supper," she said. After all these months, it was hard to imagine Pa sitting down at their table.

"So your daddy's fighting in this war, too?" asked Lt. Crumm.

Dill nodded.

The lieutenant laughed. "Ain't that the darndest thing? Here I am eating breakfast on your farm. For all we know your daddy is sitting down to eat with my family in Lexington."

"No, sir," said Dill. "My pa is in a place called Vicksburg."

Lt. Crumm shook his head. "Don't matter," he said. "We'd all be better off if we were home where we belong."

"Yes, sir," said Dill. She opened the front door. "I'm going back in the house now."

Lt. Crumm nodded.

Dill slipped through the house and out the back door, running under the eaves to Ma's vegetable garden. From behind the sweet corn she could see Lt. Crumm on the porch. The other soldiers milled about the yard, packing up their horses. When she felt sure no one was watching, she ran up the lane and dove into the woods beside Horse Creek. A pair of hands grabbed her shoulders. Dill turned to look into Simon's face. You'd've thought he was being chased by wolves to see the fear in his eyes.

"The Rebels are holding my pa and your brother at the fairgrounds," he said. "Just like the treasurer said."

"You've seen them?" asked Dill.

Simon nodded. "They're alive. But who knows what the Rebels will do to them now that they're fixing to leave Jackson."

"Is there anything we can do to set them free?" Dill asked.

"No," said Simon. "Mrs. Long talked the guards into letting her in with some coffee and biscuits. Ol' Mr. Ruf had a wad of paper money in his wallet. He was sure the Rebels'd steal it. Mrs. Long snuck the bills past the Rebels in her coffee pot."

"What's going to happen to them?" asked Dill.

"No one knows," said Simon. "They're waiting on the general to come out of the Isham House and give the next order."

"You mean General Morgan?"

Simon nodded.

"Surely he'll let them go," said Dill "He can't shoot them all."

Simon frowned. "He works for the devil. Like the rest of 'em." He gestured across Horse Creek. "You should know. Your place is crawling with them."

Dill looked across the meadow. "They're not so bad," she said. "I mean, they've eaten all our eggs and one of our hams, but they haven't set fire to anything. Two of 'em were fixing to steal one of our chickens. The lieutenant made 'em give it back."

"You have a Confederate officer camped here?" asked Simon. He pushed aside a pokeberry branch to get a better look. "Which one is he?"

"See the man in the black hat?" asked Dill.

"On your front porch?"

"Yes," said Dill. "That's Lt. Crumm." Dill pointed to the well. "See that one that's lying down over there? He has diphtheria worse than Ma. His Uncle Levi showed me how to make a poultice that brought down Ma's fever."

"To hear you talk, these Rebels are practically your family."

Dill shrugged. "Feels a bit like that," she said. "The sick soldier is no older than Jim. His uncle has a farm in Kentucky that's just like ours, except they raise horses." She looked into Simon's face. "They don't own a single slave."

Simon glared at Dill. "Your uncle must be rolling in his grave watching you feed the enemy and nurse one of them back to health."

Dill stood over Simon. "You don't know everything about this war. Our men aren't the only ones dying from Minié balls. Union soldiers're shooting 'em, too."

Simon jumped to his feet. "Who told you that?"

"Mr. Levi Long taught me all about Minié balls. A Frenchman invented them. He cursed the day they were made."

Simon pointed to the house. "Looks like the lieutenant is walking to your back door."

Dill looked across the meadow. "He probably wants more cornbread," she said. "Are you going back to town?"

"No," said Simon. "I'm staying right here to keep an eye on you."

Dill stepped across Horse Creek and walked through the middle of the Rebel camp. The soldier with the fiddle tipped his hat as she passed. By the time she got to the house, Lt. Crumm was on the back step. "I was just coming to thank you for your hospitality," he said. "We'll be leaving soon."

Dill opened the back door. Lt. Crumm's eyes fell on Jim's new riding boots. "Will you look at that?" he said. "How did you come by this fine pair of boots?"

Dill grabbed the boots. "These are my brother's," she said. "They're a gift from our pa."

The lieutenant took a boot and held it against the bottom of his foot. He pulled up a chair and sat down like he'd been invited to supper. He yanked off his old boots and dropped them to the floor. Holes the size of silver dollars were worn though the soles of both boots.

Lt. Crumm grabbed the other boot from Dill. He stepped into both boots. "How about that?" he said, getting to his feet. "It's like they were made for me." He set his foot on a chair and ran his hand over the fancy tool work in the black leather.

"They're not for you," cried Dill. "That J is for James."

The lieutenant smiled. "J is for Joshua, too." He reached into his pocket and pulled out a wad of money. "I'll pay you twenty dollars for them," he said, peeling off a bill and throwing it on the table.

Dill had seen a twenty-dollar bill, once before, when Pa had delivered two loads of hickory wood to Mr. Vaughn. The shopkeeper had paid him in cash, instead of provisions.

Lt. Crumm patted Dill's cheek. "Tell your brother his boots have a new owner."

Nellie's howl rang out from the backyard followed by a horse's whinny. "Lieutenant!" called a voice.

Dill pushed open the door. Her heart stopped. "Buck!" she yelled.

CHAPTER TWENTY-TWO

A bare-footed Rebel in patched-up pants pulled Jim's stallion into the yard. Buck stamped the ground. He shook his black mane. He snorted. The soldier beamed. "Ain't he a beauty?"

Lt. Crumm clapped the man on the shoulder. "Indeed he is," he said, running his hand down Buck's flank.

Buck threw his front legs in the air and whinnied. From across the meadow, half a dozen horses whinnied back.

"Where did you find him?" asked Lt. Crumm.

The bare-footed solider smiled. "I went lookin' for more to eat," he said. "Found me a horse in the fruit cellar."

"I beg your pardon," said Lt. Crumm. "You found *me* a horse." He took Buck's lead rope. "Sullivan! Transfer my saddle to this buckskin horse."

A short soldier in a gray uniform hurried up to the lieutenant. "Yes sir," he said, taking Buck's lead. The stallion reared up again and whinnied.

Dill leapt off the back step. "Give him to me!" she shouted.

The short soldier held the rope over Dill's head. "I'm sorry, young lady," he said. "This horse is the property of the Confederacy now."

Lt. Crumm pulled the wad of bills from his pocket again. "How much do you want for him? Fifty? A hundred?" He shoved the paper money in Dill's face.

"I won't take your money," said Dill. "Buck ain't for sale."

"The lieutenant is awfully nice to pay you," said the barefooted soldier. "At most farms, we just take horses."

"What would you say he's worth?" asked Lt. Crumm. "A hundred dollars?"

Sullivan held the rope with one hand. He held Dill away with the other as he studied Buck with the eye of a horse trader. "Twenty-five if you ask me," he said.

"Now, now," said Lt. Crumm. "Let's be fair to the young lady."

Lt. Crumm ran a hand under Buck's belly. He lifted his lips to inspect his teeth. He walked around his back side and lifted a hoof. "Looks like he's got some Kentucky thoroughbred blood," he said.

Dill shook her head. "He wasn't bred for carrying Rebels."

Lt. Crumm peeled two fifty-dollar bills off his wad and threw them at Dill's feet. "Saddle him up," he said to Sullivan.

Sullivan pulled Buck to the corner of the house and tied him to a branch of the walnut tree. Another soldier threw a blanket on his back.

Anger welled up in Dill's body as she watched Sullivan unbuckle Lt. Crumm's saddle from another horse and lift it onto Buck's back. "You lied," she shouted at the lieutenant. "You said if I cooked breakfast, you'd leave our farm the way you found it. I've been up all night making eggs and cornbread. Your men ate our biggest ham. What kind of thank-you is this?"

Lt. Crumm put his fingers to his lips and let out a whistle. "Strike camp!" he shouted. "We'll ride in thirty minutes."

The barefooted soldier pointed to the money at Dill's feet. "A hundred dollars is better than a thank-you."

Dill spat on the money. She pushed her toes against the bills and ground them into the dirt. "Your lieutenant is a thief," she said.

CHAPTER TWENTY-THREE

Dill trotted past a line of soldiers waiting at the well to fill their canteens. Around the corner of the buggy shed, Levi Long squatted beside Caleb. The red color had returned to the young soldier's face. He gasped for air.

Dill shouted at Levi. "Your lieutenant broke his promise," she said. "He's stealing Buck."

Levi Long looked puzzled. "How on earth did he find him?"

Dill wrapped a braid around her fingers. "I didn't want you to steal him. I moved him to the cellar in the night."

"A shame," said Levi Long. "No one would've found him in your spring holler."

Levi Long picked leaves off a mint sprig. "I'm sorry I can't help you, Cordelia. The boy has taken a turn for the worse. I don't see how he's leaving your farm within the hour."

Dill touched Caleb's forehead with the back of her hand. He was hotter than the night before. Levi scooped mud and spring water into a tin cup. Dill picked up a rock and mashed mint leaves. "I could run to town for the doctor," she said.

Levi stopped. "How far is your town?"

"Half a mile, as a crow flies."

"Can you get there as a crow flies?"

Dill nodded. "Our foot path is quicker than taking the road." She stopped mashing mint. "But I don't think Doc Miller can do anything more than you've already done for him."

"I'm not thinking of your doctor," said Levi Long. He took Dill by the shoulders. "Run and find the general."

Dill gasped. "General Morgan?"

Levi Long nodded. "The artillery wagon stays close by the general. Caleb can stretch out in it, underneath the cannon barrel."

Caleb coughed so hard, tears came to his eyes. Dill looked into his uncle's worried face. "How will I ever find the general?" she asked. "And even if I do find him, why would he follow me to our farm?"

Levi Long scraped the mint into the mud and stirred. "Caleb's daddy raises the fastest horses within fifty miles of Lexington," he said as he spread the poultice on his nephew's face. "If the general knew Amos Christianson's boy was sick, he'd do everything in his power to get him home."

Dill touched Caleb's hot forehead. His chest shuddered as it rose and fell. He couldn't possibly ride a horse in this condition and he was too young to leave behind. The Union Army would put him in prison where he would surely die.

Dill thought about how Uncle Swinge would've felt if this had been Jim. Her heart leapt at a thought. She turned to Levi Long. "General Morgan is holding my brother at the county fairgrounds. Do you think he'd turn him loose if I asked?"

"He might," said Levi Long. "He has a soft heart. Run and find him."

Dill dashed back to the house. She passed men rolling up bedrolls and packing horses. Behind the house, Buck stamped at the end of his reins. Lt. Crumm's man, Sullivan, was nowhere to be seen. Dill could untie Buck and ride him to Jackson. But a horse like Buck would only distract the general.

Inside the house, Ma's breathing was raspy as she slept. There was no need to wake her. Dill frowned at the image of herself in Ma's mirror. Dirt covered her cheeks. Her braids, which Ma always kept so neat, had fallen to ruin.

She dipped a rag in the basin and wiped her face. There was no time to retie her braids. The yellow scarf was still in its spot in the cedar chest. Dill folded the silk in a triangle and threw it over her head. She tied the ends under her chin. Such a fine scarf looked silly with her old dress and dirty pinafore, but it would have to do. She had no time to change.

Nellie jumped to her feet and followed Dill around the house. At the edge of the garden, Dill knelt down. "Stay here," she said. "Protect Ma and the farm."

Nellie pulled her ears tight against her head. Her one brown eye begged to come along.

"No," said Dill. "You have to stay."

Nellie tucked her tail between her legs and turned back to the house. Dill could see the line of soldiers at the well growing shorter. As soon as Lt. Crumm gave the order, the Rebels would ride off, with or without Caleb. Dill turned and raced down the path to Jackson.

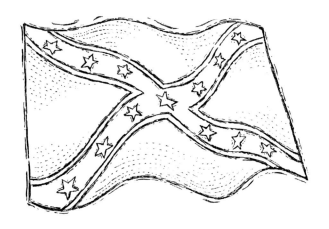

CHAPTER TWENTY-FOUR

The fringes of Ma's silk scarf bounced against Dill's chest as her feet pounded the path. One spring morning not long ago, she had followed Jim down this same path to witness the mustering of the Ohio 53rd on Jackson's town square. Uncle Swinge had looked so handsome in his blue uniform. What would he think of her now, running to town to search for a general dressed in gray?

Blackberry branches grabbed at Dill's pinafore. Her hand brushed a clump of nettles. She spit on the stinging skin and kept running.

The path turned away from the creek and up the hill, opening into a clearing. Ahead of her stood the white frame houses along Water Street. From Water Street she turned onto Broadway. The *clop-clop* of horses' hooves signaled a company of soldiers trotting down Main. Dill dropped behind a clump of bushes. A line of soldiers dressed in gray turned down Broadway. Except for the color of their uniforms, they looked every bit like the company of soldiers that had ridden out of Jackson just two years before. That company had carried the stars and stripes.

A rider leading the gray company carried a pole with a red square. Across the square was a blue X filled with white stars – a Rebel flag.

Dill could feel her heart beating in her chest. If she did nothing, this company of Rebels would never know she was there. She thought of Jim imprisoned at the fairgrounds and Caleb's gut splitting coughs. The Rebel flag in the front row loomed larger as the line of men approached.

Dill leapt into the road. The soldier carrying the flag jerked his reins. His horse pranced sideways, bumping into the next rider's horse.

"Stupid girl," shouted the flag carrier. "You could've been trampled."

Dill wrapped the fringes of Ma's yellow scarf around her fingers. "I was sent to find the general," she said.

The soldier shoved his hat back to get a better look at Dill. "Are you askin' for General Morgan?" he asked.

"Yes," said Dill. "I have to speak with him."

The soldier scowled. "That's him, right there," he said, pointing to the man in the center of the next row of riders. "But what does a little girl want with the likes of a general?"

There was no time to answer such a foolish question. Dill dipped under the flag and past the soldier. When she looked up again, she was standing before a line of handsome men on tall horses. They wore freshly pressed uniforms with every brass button sewn in place. Dill looked into the squinting eyes of a soldier with a waxed mustache. The brim of his hat shaded his face. A feather the length of Nellie's tail soared above the hat, curving over his shoulder. His silver sword touched the tops of his black boots.

Dill stepped in front of the gentleman's horse. "I'm here to fetch the general," she said.

The handsome soldier tipped the brim of his black hat. His gray eyes held not the slightest hint of anger. "To what do I owe this acquaintance, young Miss?"

"Are you General Morgan?" asked Dill.

The soldier smiled. "Indeed I am."

Dill had never met a general. She wondered if she should curtsey. "Levi Long sent me," she said, bowing her head.

General Morgan smiled. "Yes," he said. "I know the gentleman of whom you speak." He turned to the soldier beside him. "Sergeant Long is in Crumm's company."

The general's reaction gave Dill hope. "Lt. Crumm and his men are camped at our farm," she said. "Sgt. Long asked me to come find you."

The general frowned. "Is Levi in trouble?"

Dill shook her head. "It's his nephew. He's sick with diphtheria."

The general's eyebrows scrunched to a knot. "Do you mean Caleb?"

"Yes sir," said Dill. "Sgt. Long wants you to come to our farm."

General Morgan turned to the soldier on his left. "That's Amos Christianson's boy." The other man nodded. "Tell me more," said the general.

Dill's heart rose to think General Morgan might give a lick about Caleb. "Lt. Crumm is fixing to saddle up his men. But Sgt. Long and me, we don't see how Caleb can ride. He's burning up with fever and he hasn't had more than a sip of water in two days."

General Morgan ran his fingers to the end of his waxed mustache. He turned in his saddle. "Baxter!" he called. "Bring me that little mare we picked up in Piketon. I have a rider for her."

Dill shook her head. "You don't understand. Caleb is too sick to ride."

The lines around the general's gray eyes crinkled. "The little mare isn't for Caleb," he said. "She's for you."

CHAPTER TWENTY-FIVE

A soldier trotted up with a chocolate brown mare tied to his saddle horn. He untied the mare's reins and handed them to General Morgan.

"I apologize for not offering a proper saddle to a lady as lovely as yourself," said General Morgan. He reached the reins down to Dill.

Dill took the reins. "Thank you, General," she said. "I s'pect I can ride bareback."

"Get the little lady onto the mare," said the general, "so we can move along."

The soldier to the general's left climbed off his horse and offered his hands as a step. Dill hopped up to sit on the mare. The general turned to the soldier on his right. "Duke," he said. "Take your men and ride on to Keystone while I check on Amos's boy."

"Caleb can't sit up," said Dill. "He'll need a wagon."

"Leave us the artillery wagon," General Morgan shouted to Duke.

"There's one more thing," said Dill.

General Morgan raised an eyebrow.

"I hear your men are holding my brother at the fairgrounds. Could you see it in your heart to set him free? My pa is at war and I don't know how we'll manage without him."

A smile spread across the general's face. "I've already taken care of him," he said. "All of your town's men will be turned loose in thirty minutes, after the last of my soldiers has fled Jackson."

Dill's heart soared. It was all she could do not to jump off the horse and hug the general. "Thank you," she said.

General Morgan tipped his hat. "Show us to your farm, young lady."

Dill untied her scarf and wrapped it around the reins. She kicked her heels into the little mare's side and galloped ahead of the general's company.

Dill should've felt proud to lead a general up her lane, but all she felt was worry as she trotted into the yard. Nellie howled at the sight of General Morgan.

"Hush!" shouted Dill. The beagle sniffed the air then ran beside the chocolate mare.

Crumm's ragged soldiers snapped to attention at the sight of General Morgan. The barefooted soldier who had raided the cellar gave a brisk salute.

Lt. Crumm strode up to the general. "Sir," he said, with a salute. "To what do I owe this visit?"

General Morgan returned the lieutenant's salute. "This little lady tells me Caleb Christianson is ill."

Lt. Crumm's eyes grew round at the sight of Dill on the chocolate mare. "Miss Cordelia," he gasped. "How did you come across General Morgan?"

Dill slid off the mare's back. "I went looking for him." She turned to General Morgan. "Follow me," she said.

Levi Long squatted beside a pair of boots sticking up from a gray blanket. Caleb's neck was swollen twice as big as the night before, his face flushed.

"Levi!" shouted General Morgan. "What's wrong with Amos's boy?"

"He's picked a devil of a time to come down with diphtheria," said Levi Long. He gave Caleb's shoulder a soft shake.

The boy's blue eyes flicked open. He tried to lift his head off the ground. "General," he whispered.

General Morgan put his finger to Caleb's lips. "Save your energy, son." He turned to Levi. "What can we do for him?"

"We can't put him in a saddle," said Levi.

Lt. Crumm bent over Caleb. "Has the infirmary wagon left town?" he asked.

"It's headed east with Duke," said General Morgan. He gestured to a horse and wagon in Dill's front yard. "We can make room in the artillery wagon." He touched the cracked mud on Caleb's swollen neck. "What's this on the boy?"

"Mixture of mud and mint leaves," said Levi Long. "This young lady led me to the mint. She brought down Caleb's fever so he could sleep."

General Morgan pushed his hat off his forehead and looked around the yard. "You picked a lovely hollow to rest for the night," he said to Lt. Crumm. "Reminds me a bit of your farm." He winked at Dill. "You even found a pretty young lady to tend to our sick."

Lt. Crumm nodded. "The girl fixed our breakfast," he said. "I didn't know about her nursing skills."

Blam!

A tree branch cracked above the buggy shed. Oak leaves fluttered to the general's feet.

"Good Lord," said General Morgan. "Someone is shooting at us."

A thin wisp of smoke hung in the air beside the barn. Lt. Crumm turned to Sullivan. "Find the man who fired that shot."

A clump of blond hair appeared in the loft window. Dill gasped. "It's Simon," she shouted. "Get down!"

The barrel of Grandpap's flintlock pointed at the buggy shed.

Blam!

A pair of robins squawked and flew over their heads.

"Hurry," said Dill. "Before he reloads."

Sullivan raced into the barnyard with two gray soldiers at his heels. Simon's face appeared at the window. He jammed a rod down the musket barrel before lifting the wooden stock to his cheek.

A gray figure appeared behind Simon. Seconds later, the gun barrel swung wildly, pointing to the sky.

Blam!

Simon's face disappeared. Dill could hear scuffling in the barn. Sullivan appeared in the window. He held tight to Simon's white shirt, dangling him out the window. Simon kicked and punched the air. "Let me go!" he shouted.

A soldier behind Sullivan held up Grandpap's rabbit shooter. "We've got his gun," he called.

Lt. Crumm scowled at Dill. "You little wretch," he said. "You planned this plot on the general's life."

"I didn't," said Dill, her heart racing. "I brought the general to help Caleb."

General Morgan waved a hand at Lt. Crumm. "I believe the young lady," he said. "She meant no harm to me."

Simon marched down the path ahead of the Rebels. His hands were tied behind his back. His face wore a frown. Sullivan nodded to a man standing beside Buck. The soldier stepped forward with a rope as big around as his arm, a loop tied in one end.

"Oh no," gasped Dill. "Not a hangman's noose."

Sullivan threw the loop over Simon's head and cinched the knot around his neck. The blood drained from Simon's face.

"Put the boy on my horse," said Lt. Crumm.

"Wait!" cried Dill. "Simon is a good shot. General Morgan would be dead if he'd meant to take his life."

Sullivan led Simon to the walnut tree. He and the barefooted soldier lifted him into Lt. Crumm's black saddle. Sullivan hurled the long end of the rope over a sturdy branch and tugged until the knot rose over Simon's head.

Lt. Crumm shook a finger at Simon. "Now you will see how we punish Yankees who try to kill our general."

Simon's teeth chattered. "I shot over his head," he said. "Really. I didn't intend to kill him."

Dill took hold of General Morgan's hand. "I beg you," she pleaded. "Don't let them hang Simon."

"You obviously know this scoundrel," said General Morgan.

"I've known him all my life," said Dill. "He's a foolish boy, but he's not a murderer." She turned to Lt. Crumm. "Show Simon's gun to the general."

Lt. Crumm took the flintlock from Sullivan and put it in General Morgan's hands. A smile spread across the general's face. "My grandfather had a gun like this," he said, "from the old country."

Dill touched the wooden stock. "A fellow couldn't hit the side of a barn with this old musket." Dill pointed at Simon. "He said so himself."

Simon squirmed in the saddle. "I said *you* couldn't hit the side of a barn."

Dill ignored Simon. "Won't you let him go?" she asked. "He doesn't deserve to die."

Little lines appeared at the corners of General Morgan's eyes. He laughed. "Get the boy off the horse," he said. "We'll leave it to this young lady to dole out his punishment."

Sullivan pulled Simon off of Buck and lifted the rope off his neck. He walked him to the house, making him sit on the back step. Lt. Crumm looked down on Dill. "Keep him tied up," he said, "until we're gone."

General Morgan stuck a foot in his stirrup and swung up into his saddle. "Thank you, Little Lady, for taking care of my men." He shouted to the driver of the artillery wagon. "Can you make room for a sick boy?"

"I've already piled up straw," said the driver. "Bring him over."

Dill squatted beside Caleb. "Rest now, and get better. Your mother doesn't want you coming home in a coffin."

Caleb nodded. "I'll never forget your kindness," he said in a whisper.

Levi Long and Sullivan picked up the corners of Caleb's gray blanket and lifted him into the bed of the wagon. Levi handed Caleb his canteen and backpack.

Dill marched over to Lt. Crumm. "I kept my end of our bargain," she said. "Now you keep yours. Let me keep my horse."

Lt. Crumm's eyes narrowed. "Your friend got to keep his life," he said. "That's payment enough."

Levi Long stepped before the general's horse. "With all due respect, General Morgan," he said. "Miss Cordelia cooked breakfast for our company. She cared for Caleb even as her own mother was suffering from diphtheria inside the house. Do you think we could spare her brother's horse?"

Dill picked the lieutenant's money out of the dirt and gave it to the general. "The lieutenant is wearing my brother's boots," she said. "He left this money for Jim's horse. I don't care about the boots or the money. I just want Buck."

General Morgan turned to the lieutenant. "Joshua?" he asked. "What's all this fuss about?"

"It's about the buckskin stallion," said Lt. Crumm. "A mighty fine horse."

The general looked across the yard at Buck. "He's a beauty all right." He turned back to Lt. Crumm. "Let the girl keep him."

Crumm snapped a salute to the general. "Sullivan!" he shouted. "Remove my saddle."

CHAPTER TWENTY-SIX

Dill ran a hand down Buck's soft muzzle. She reached under his belly and unbuckled Lt. Crumm's saddle. Sullivan pulled off the saddle. He removed the bridle and returned Buck's worn halter. Dill wrapped the lead rope around her hand.

"Never thought I'd see the lieutenant give such a fine horse back to a Yankee," said the barefooted soldier.

Dill smiled up at General Morgan. "Thank you," she said.

The general tipped his hat. "Carry on," he said to Lt. Crumm.

The lieutenant put his fingers to his lips. His whistle echoed off Cemetery Hill. "Move out," he called.

Next to the buggy shed, Levi Long cinched his bedroll to his saddle. Bits of dried mud filled the cracks around his fingernails.

"Thank you for helping me keep Buck," said Dill.

"Now see here, young lady. You earned the right to keep that horse." He patted Dill's cheek. "Thank you for helping my sister's boy. You're a brave little lady, Miss Cordelia."

Dill twisted a braid around her fingers. "I s'pect you ought to call me Dill," she said, "like my family."

Levi Long tipped his hat. "Thank you for your kindness, Miss Dill." He threw a leg over his horse and trotted after the other soldiers. Caleb's coughs filled the back of the wagon as it disappeared down the lane.

Simon squirmed on the back step. "Can you untie me?"

Dill tied Buck to a low branch of the walnut tree. She shook her head at Simon. "What were you thinking, shooting at the general like that?" She loosened the rope around his hands.

Simon rubbed his wrists. "I was looking out for Jim," he said. "He didn't spend all that time breaking Buck so some thieving Rebel could steal him."

Dill laughed. "After all your fear of dying, you almost got yourself hung."

Simon's blue eyes sparkled. "I expect you're right," he said, laughing. He walked up the steps. "Did the Rebels leave anything to eat?"

Dill pushed past Simon. "Can you wait 'til I check on Ma?"

"I s'pose," said Simon. "But I'm awfully hungry."

Dill hurried down the hall. She couldn't wait to tell Ma about Jim. Her heart swelled knowing he was safe.

Ma's room was as quiet as night. Her breathing was soft, no longer raspy. She slept without coughing. Dill closed Ma's door.

"I set aside an egg and a couple squares of cornbread for my own breakfast," Dill said in the kitchen. "I'll share them with you."

Simon stood beside the table holding a dusty boot. "Look at this," he said, sticking his finger through a hole in the bottom. "Jim couldn't have worn holes through these boots already."

Dill set two plates on the table. "Those are Lt. Crumm's," she said. "He took Jim's boots."

"I knew he was a thief," said Simon, dropping the boot. It clunked on the hardwood floor.

"He's not a thief," said Dill. She picked up the lieutenant's money and waved it in front of Simon. "He paid me for Jim's boots."

Simon grabbed the paper bill. "This is Confederate money. It's useless on this side of the river."

Dill took the twenty-dollar bill from Simon. Sure enough; it said Confederate States of America across the front. A hot feeling spread up her neck and across her face. "I've been tricked," she said.

"After we eat, you'd better look around to see what else he stole from you." Simon spread molasses on his cornbread. He took a bite and frowned. "Hey," he said, sticking his fingers in his mouth. "There's eggshell in this cornbread."

A laugh rose up from Dill's stomach and burst out her lips sending yellow crumbs across the table. She laughed so hard, tears streamed down her cheeks.

Simon stuck his fingers in his mouth again. He pulled out a piece of eggshell as big as his thumbnail. "What's so funny?"

"The eggshell," said Dill. "It was meant for the Rebels."

Nellie's howl came through the open window. Dill ran through the parlor. "It's your pa. He's got Jim with him!"

Jim ran up the porch steps and kissed the front door. "I never thought I'd see this house again," he said. "How's Ma?"

"Better," said Dill. "She practically slept through the Rebels."

"Rebels? Here?" asked Mr. Harrison. "What about our farm?"

Simon poked his head out the front door. "It's all right, Pa," he said. "A pack of Rebels came through. They left when they discovered we were out of food. It was nothing like what happened here. Dill must've had a hundred of 'em camped on her farm."

Jim's face turned white. "A hundred Rebels?"

"Simon's exaggerating," said Dill. "There were only fifty-two."

Jim looked at the piles of horse manure dotting the yard. "It looks like all fifty-two horses passed through our front yard."

"Fifty-three if you count the general's horse," said Simon.

Jim scratched his head. "General Morgan was here on our farm? When?"

"A short while ago," said Dill.

Jim sat down on the bench. "The general freed us a short while ago. But not 'til he scared the daylights out of us by marching us to town and threatening us with a firing squad." He took off his hat and scratched his head. "I wonder what brought him to our farm."

Mr. Harrison picked up his reins. "I'm going to check on our place. Simon? Are you coming?"

Simon shook his head. "Not 'til I raid Dill's cellar."

Ma's voice called from the bedroom. "Jim? Is that you?"

Dill hurried into Ma's room. She lifted the rag off her mother's forehead and dipped it in the basin. Ma smiled up at Jim in the doorway. "You're home," she whispered.

Jim nodded. "How're you feelin'?"

"Better, now that you're safe," she said. She closed her eyes and breathed slow and steady.

Dill stepped out and closed the door. She followed Jim down the hall. In the kitchen, Simon lifted the wax plug off a crock of Ma's strawberry preserves.

"Simon!" said Dill. "Can't you wait to be invited?"

Simon shook his head. Jam dripped from the corners of his mouth.

Jim picked up a dusty boot. "These aren't my boots," he said.

Simon waved the lieutenant's money. "Dill sold your boots to the Rebels."

"I did nothing of the kind," said Dill. "Lt. Crumm tried on your boots. When they fit, he gave me twenty dollars for them. You can't blame him. Look at the holes in the bottom of his."

Jim took the twenty-dollar bill. "But this is Confederate money."

The blood rushed to Dill's face again. "I'll take it to Mr. Vaughn. Maybe he can trade it across the river."

Simon grabbed the money. "I told you they were thieves."

"What else did they steal?" asked Jim.

"Dill fed 'em breakfast," said Simon.

Dill glared at Simon. "No thanks to you." She turned to Jim. "They found Buck. The lieutenant saddled him up. He gave me a hundred dollars for him."

"Rebel money," said Simon.

Jim ran to the back door. Buck grazed in the shadow of the walnut tree. "But he's still here," he said. "What made him change his mind?"

"General Morgan made the lieutenant give him back," said Dill. "He figured I'd earned the right to keep him by feeding his soldiers, and caring for a sick one." Dill thought of Caleb. She hoped he was comfortable in the back of the artillery wagon.

A strange look came across Jim's face. He marched out the back door, stopping to untie Buck. "Come to the barn," he called over his shoulder.

Nellie led the way up the path. "You're in trouble now," said Simon, trotting to keep up with Dill. "He's going to teach you a lesson for almost losing Buck."

Dill's mind raced. What was her brother fixing to teach her?

CHAPTER TWENTY-SEVEN

Simon followed Dill to Buck's stall. Jim and Buck weren't there.

"Jim?" called Dill.

"Out here," Jim shouted.

Sure enough; there was Jim in the outer lot. He was saddling Buck. "Where are you going?" asked Dill.

"I'm not going anywhere," said Jim. "It's time you got that ride I've been promising."

Dill wrapped her arms around Jim. "Now?" she asked.

Jim grinned. "Can you think of a better time?"

Simon stomped his foot in the dirt. "I wanted the first ride."

Jim punched Simon's shoulder. "Stop your whining," he said. "You'll get your turn. After Dill."

Jim boosted Dill into the saddle. "Open the gate," he said to Simon.

Simon swung open the gate.

"Don't fall off," said Jim. "Or Ma will take a switch to me."

Dill kicked her feet. Buck galloped out the gate and up the lane. Dill could feel his muscles tighten and loosen as he raced along the cornfields, down the road and straight to the top of Cemetery Hill.

At the cedar grove, Dill pulled back on the reins forcing Buck to walk past Uncle Swinge. She let out the reins by the giant sycamore. Buck trotted up to the Jones Family plot and stopped. The air was clear enough to see beyond Pike Hill.

A stiff breeze filled Dill's face. She patted Buck's slender neck. "We're as close as you can get to heaven," she said.

Author's Note

In July of 1863, General John Hunt Morgan and two thousand Confederate soldiers raided across Indiana and Ohio for eighteen days. They ripped out telegraph lines, robbed banks, and burned bridges all in an effort to divert Union forces from the South and frighten the Yankees.

General Morgan and his men stopped to rest for nearly twelve hours in Jackson County, Ohio where fifty Rebel raiders camped on my great grandparents' farm. My father's great aunt, Cordelia "Dill" Dunbar, was nine years old when she cooked breakfast for the enemy soldiers. Her entire family was sick with diphtheria.

After the war, the Dunbar family moved to Southern Indiana where Aunt Cordelia lived a long and happy life. She delighted in sharing the story of fixing breakfast for Morgan's Raiders with her many nieces and nephews. My father, Robert Trimble, was one of Dill's great-nephews. He and his brothers, Rush and Ralph, passed her story down to their children including my brother, John, and me. We have told her story to our own children, Dill's great, great, great nieces and nephews. Thus, this family legend lives on.

Rebel Raiders is a fictionalized version of Aunt Cordelia's story. Every event is based on a true incident that occurred somewhere along the route of Morgan's Raid, many in Jackson County.

For more information on this story and the author go to www.rebelraiders.us.

Acknowledgements

I thank my brother, John C. Trimble, who planted the seed for *Rebel Raiders* by suggesting I write about our great, great Aunt Cordelia's story. Many people provided encouragement along the way. Others filled in historical details. Still others read and re-read the story and suggested changes. I couldn't have written this novel without them.

For historical support, I thank Amy Landrum, Robert Ervin, Ren Fenik, Dick Skidmore, Chris Graham, Bruce Bybee of the John M. Browning Firearms Museum, and my father, Bob Trimble, whose childhood farm memories were priceless. I also thank Mrs. Kathryn Loxley for showing me around *The Shire*, her lovely Jackson County farm.

I'm grateful for early readers including Cathy Signorelli, Heidi Roemer, Patricia Lee Gauch, Kendra Marcus, Jane Stevens Simons, Nancy Parks, Kitty McKoon-Hennick, Bonnie Baxter, Jane Campbell, Cooper Dean, Bob and Barbara Trimble, Laura Trimble Elbogen, Megan Pedersen, Barbara Fricke, Bobbie Pyron, and Elizabeth Walker.

I'm grateful for later readers including Shawn Newell, Lyn Christian, Kaylee McHugh, Sydney Salter Husseman, Kelley Lindberg, Jean Reagan, Becky Hall, Chris Graham, and Bobbie Pyron.

Thank you to Dana Tumpowsky for her copyediting skills and to Hazel Mitchell for her beautiful illustrations which grace the cover and begin each chapter.

And finally, I offer my love and gratitude to my husband and sons, Dave, Dan and Charlie Actor, for persevering through many years and countless revisions of this novel.

CPSIA information can be obtained at www.ICGtesting.com
Printed in the USA
LVOW080337060413

327924LV00002B/185/P